THE VOYNICH GAMBIT

A Norman Blalock Mystery

I0545165

Quintin Peterson

ᑫℙ Ram Press

THE VOYNICH GAMBIT

ISBN: 978-0-9891369-1-4

Cover Design by **The Cover Collection**, United Kingdom

Printed in the U.S.A.

 **Ram Press**
Washington, D.C.

For Reggie Young

All the world's a stage,
And all the men and women merely players;
They have their exits and their entrances,
And one man in his time plays many parts.

– William Shakespeare's *As You Like It*, Act II, Scene VII

ROOFTOP OF THE FOLGER SHAKESPEARE LIBRARY
CAPITOL HILL
WASHINGTON, D.C.

HALLOWEEN

21:11 Hours

Lt. Norman Blalock speed-dialed Satō. When the Japanese businessman answered, he said. "Deposit the balance now."

"What?" Satō asked. "But, I've already deposited the balance. Ms. Netram contacted me a little while ago and gave me another account number. What is going on?"

"Just a miscommunication," Blalock lied. "We'll be in touch."

Blalock discontinued the phone call and hissed, "Dirty bitch!" Kavitha Netram had screwed him on this side-deal.

He pulled from his pants pocket a second burner, the same model as his personal cell phone, and worked the Smartphone's keys; he had to conduct his banking transactions swiftly so he would not be cut out of the main deal, too.

Afterward, Blalock made his way down from the roof, to the third floor. He turned right and hurried down the hall past the Werner Gundersheimer Conservation Laboratory on his left, and then ducked into Mechanical Room #7, located at the opposite end of the hall from the "ART DEPT." He ran up the stairs to Catwalk #1 and ran toward the door at the other end.

"Where are you going, lieutenant?"

Lt. Blalock stopped in his tracks and turned to find muscle-bound, platinum blonde Armed Response Team Sgt.

Lou Carew standing at the top of the stairs the lieutenant had just used to get to the catwalk.

Sgt. Carew smiled and held out his iPhone. "You're Lojacked."

"So it's you, huh?" Lt. Blalock asked. "When did she get to you?"

Sgt. Carew chuckled and walked toward Lt. Blalock. "Boy, have you got the wrong guy. Rupert is my friend."

Lt. Blalock shook his head. "It's always you big, muscle-bound he-men, isn't it?"

"Cut the crap, old man. Give it to me."

"I don't have it," said Blalock, backing away. "The jewelry box was empty…"

"Bullshit!" Sgt. Carew yelled. "Give it to me and you won't get hurt."

"Why don't you shoot me and take it?"

"I don't need a gun to take you out," Sgt. Carew assured him.

"Shoot me or beat me to death, it doesn't make much difference," Lt. Blalock said. "You can't get away with it so long as I'm alive."

"Then you'll have to die," Sgt. Carew said flatly.

Sgt. Carew ran toward Lt. Blalock.

As soon as Carew was within striking distance, Blalock punched him in his windpipe. The behemoth stopped in his tracks, clutching his throat with both hands, gasping for air.

"I guess Rupert didn't tell you I have a black belt in Karate," said Blalock. "Maybe he didn't know."

Blalock closed the distance between him and the door at the other end of Catwalk #1. He opened the door and then turned around to climb down the ladder at that end, only to find the still gasping Sgt. Carew had closed the distance as well, and was reaching for Norman. Carew grabbed his sweater and when he jerked free, Blalock lost his footing and fell to the floor below, just outside of Mechanical Room #5.

2

He heard bones in his right ankle snap and instantly felt white hot pain.

As he grimaced, Lt. Blalock looked up and saw the face of the now unconscious Sgt. Carew hanging over the doorframe at the top of the ladder. Blalock stood and, wincing all the way, opened the door to Mechanical Room #5 and went in. He quickly found a toolbox, opened it, and found duct tape inside. With alacrity, he wrapped duct tape around and around his broken ankle to give it some support and then cut his makeshift bandage free from the roll with a box cutter he also found in the toolbox and then cut two strips about 8 inches in length and attached them to the back of his hand to use later...

Blalock tossed the box cutter back into toolbox then removed the back from the "ghost phone" Whyte had supplied him. He removed the iPhone's battery, took out its SIM card, and crushed it under the boot heel of his good foot. Afterward, he put Whyte's iPhone back together, picked up the shattered SIM card and tossed it into a huge trash can full of industrial rubbish. Wincing with every hop-step, he then exited Mechanical Room #5, turned left, and walked past the Elizabethan Theatre's control booth and took the steps down from the third floor of the theatre to backstage, where he wiped all of his fingerprints off all sides of the ghost phone using the front of his sweater and then tossed Whyte's burner into a box of props.

Lt. Blalock peeked from backstage to make sure the theatre was empty. It was; it was intermission and all the patrons were out in the Great Hall, where concessions were on sale...

Norman keyed his radio and said, "Adam-3 to Central."

"Go ahead for Central," SPO Luther Cary's voice came over the radio.

"Fire and Water Watches complete," said Blalock. "All clear in the art vault and east and west wings secure."

"10-4," SPO Cary said. "At 21:17 hours."

Blalock exited the Elizabethan Theatre and hobbled into the theatre lobby.

"What's wrong with your leg?" SPO Swann asked.

"Oh, I just sprained my ankle," Lt. Blalock lied. "Tripped coming down the stairs."

"You look terrible," said Swann. "You're sweating. You should go to the infirmary."

"I'm on my way now," Blalock said.

Norman walked into the Great Hall and made his way through the crowd of theatergoers who were buying and consuming concessions during the intermission for *Othello* and then entered the Gail Paster Reading Room via the unlocked east double metal and glass door, the one he'd opened earlier to accommodate a wheelchair-bound patron and allow him access to the theatre.

Sgt. Lou Carew made his way through the crowd, following him...

[0000]

Blalock, perspiring and breathing heavily, had paused and looked at the portraits of Henry Clay and Emily Folger painted by renowned artist Frank O. Salisbury in 1927, located in the Gail Paster Reading Room, under a replica of William Shakespeare's tomb and straddling the back wall with the columbarium niche containing the Folgers' urns concealed behind a brass plaque with an etched crucifix above the inscription:

TO THE GLORY OF
WILLIAM SHAKESPEARE
AND THE GREATER GLORY
OF GOD

HENRY CLAY FOLGER
JUNE 18 1857
JUNE 11 1930

EMILY CLARA JORDAN FOLGER
MAY 15 1858
FEBRUARY 21 1936

Suddenly, his left arm went numb and he felt excruciating pain in his chest, as though his heart were being gripped in a vise. He took his radio from his Sam Browne belt, keyed it, but could not speak. He dropped his radio and collapsed to the carpeted floor.

Not now, Norman thought…

[0000]

Kavitha Netram was sitting in the Gift Shop, checking her watch, when there was the sound of breaking glass coming from the hallway of the Authorized Personnel Only section nearby.

"What the…," SPO Luther Cary exclaimed.

Just then, the message came over the radio: "Adam-69 to Central, have someone respond to the Old Reading Room with the AED ASAP and call an ambulance. Blalock is down and I'm starting CPR."

"Central copy," SPO Cary spoke into the radio. "Any available Adam unit to assist."

"Adam-21 copy!" a voice came over the radio.

SPO Cary picked up the receiver on the desk phone and dialed 9-1-1.

Kavitha declared, "I'm CPR trained."

Her knee-high black leather high-heel boots clicking like cat claws on the slate floor, she ran to the door of the Registrar's Office and noticed broken glass underfoot and

5

observed an octagonal section of glass cleanly cut within the borders of one of the octagon designs on the glass door was missing. It was curious, but she had no time to ponder it. Kavitha opened the door and ran through the office, through the double wood and glass doors and into the Gail Paster Reading Room.

Kavitha found a big and beefy platinum blonde guard wearing snug-fitting navy blue BDU's kneeling beside Norman.

"Get the AED," she told the muscle-bound guard. "I'm CPR trained."

Lou Carew aka Adam-69 stood and ran from the room, a Heckler & Koch MP5 submachine gun dangling from a strap slung over his right shoulder.

Kavitha ran to Norman where he lay near the back wall, in close proximity to the Folgers' urns entombed in a columbarium niche behind a memorial plaque straddled by portraits of Henry Clay and Emily. Before she started CPR, Kavitha quickly checked Blalock's shirt and pants pockets, but did not find the BlackBerry, only his cell phone, the mourning rings, and his personal keys in his pants pockets. She left the cell phone where it was, but hid the rings in her bra and put Norman's keys inside her left boot. Then she went to work on him.

When Adam-69 returned with the Automated External Defibrillator (AED), SPO Donnell Curtis on his heels, she continued CPR until Adam-69 was ready to use the AED. Adam-69 removed the AED from its case and turned it on. The AED spoke: *Begin by removing all clothing from the patient's chest...*

SPO Curtis told Kavitha to back away and then quickly pulled Blalock's sweater over his head and off his arms and tossed it. He then ripped open Blalock's shirt, sending buttons flying in all directions, and used scissors to cut Blalock's tee shirt up the middle. Adam-69 applied the electrodes to Blalock's chest, making certain that the adhesive backed pads were securely affixed.

AED: *"Stand clear. No one should touch the patient. Analyzing heart rhythm. Shock advised..."*

"Clear!" Adam-69 yelled.

Kavitha was dismayed, yet her mind was reeling. She stared at the portraits of the Folgers on the back wall as she considered what she was going to tell Mr. Whyte about this fiasco.

The writing table was not on Blalock, but Whyte would believe there were only two possibilities: either Blalock had hidden the writing table somewhere in the building or she had stolen it from Blalock as he lay dying on the floor of the Gail Paster Reading Room in order to broker her own deal for its sale to one of his competitors behind his back. Therefore, she would forever be under his scrutiny.

Maybe in the end Norman had not trusted them...*her*, after all; maybe he'd decided not to give the artifact to them until he could be sure of his safety and had in fact hidden it somewhere. But she didn't believe so. She was certain that she had had Norman wrapped around her little finger, that he had had no idea that part of her contract was to kill him once Shakespeare's BlackBerry was in hand...at which time Whyte, with the help of the president of the Swiss bank he'd referred Norman to, would withdraw the funds from Norm's account and redeposit the money in his own. S.O.P. And cracking that Cracker Jack box of an antique floor safe of Norman's in his basement, which she was certain Norman didn't know she knew about, and retrieving the negotiable bearer bonds and cash would have been a snap for her.

Regardless, she would never reveal to Whyte that she felt guilty about setting Norman up; nor that she believed the Folgers themselves somehow had orchestrated Blalock's demise from beyond the grave and had taken the writing table. Furthermore, she would never divulge that she was certain the Folger Shakespeare Library had the best security anywhere and any attempt to defile this institution would prove futile.

Intuition informed her that security personnel there are not the only ones guarding Shakespeare.

At first, she couldn't quite put her finger on the feeling that was quickly overcoming her and then she was struck by the starting revelation that it was remorse that she was feeling. There's a first time for everything.

She was also astonished to learn that she was going to miss him. At the very moment she realized this, Norman stirred and started coughing and Kavitha's heart leapt.

AED: *"Shock not recommended..."*

Lou Carew jumped to his feet. "I'm going to go check on that ambulance."

SPO Carew ran from the Gail Paster Reading Room, but stopped in the Registrar's Office. He pulled out his cell phone and speed-dialed a number. He put the phone to his ear, waited a few moments and then said, "He didn't have it on him."

"You're kidding, Lou," Rupert Whyte said on the other end. "You got to him first, didn't you?"

"Yes," SPO Carew said. "It wasn't on him. He must have hid it. He had a heart attack, but he's coming around. We'll make him tell us where it is."

Whyte disconnected the phone call.

"Rupert?" Carew said. "Rupert?"

SPO Carew put away his cell phone and ran to the west lobby. Just as he arrived, recently fired Officer James Moll, armed with a Colt .45 semiautomatic pistol and wearing camouflage BDUs, war paint, and his new hairdo, cornrows flowing down his back, the seashells on the tips of each extension clacking together as they swished from one shoulder to the other, entered through Door 49. Carew instantly raised and aimed his MP5 submachine gun. SPO Luther Cary ducked and reached for one of the hidden pistols in the guard's desk just as Sgt. Carew and James Moll opened fire on each other.

Sgt. Carew fired bullets into James Moll that struck from his belly button to his forehead and Moll's one shot struck Carew square in the forehead. Both simultaneously dropped to the slate floor like sacks of potatoes.

SPO Cary, gun in hand, went to Moll and kicked away his weapon from his dead hand. He then got on the desk phone and once again dialed 9-1-1.

Kavitha ran down the stairs to the gift shop offices, retrieved her belongings, and then exited through Door 21, a restricted entrance in back of the library. There she met Satō, where they exchanged the mourning rings that were the key to unlocking the secret compartment of the jewelry box in the Folger's Babette Craven Art Vault where the priceless artifact Mr. Whyte sought was supposedly hidden. (Kavitha and Norman had cut a side-deal with him to sell him Rupert Whyte's mourning rings and replace them with replicas, because Satō believed that he had the true jewelry box, which required three, not two, mourning rings to access its secret compartment. There was no downside to playing it both ways.)

Satō went his way and she went in the opposite direction, toward 3rd Street, where she was scheduled to meet with Rupert Whyte. At East Capitol and 3rd Street she climbed into the back of Whyte's limo, which was parked on the N.E. side of East Capitol.

"What happened?" Rupert Whyte asked.

"A guard was in a shootout with an ex-security officer, James Moll. Moll went insane and got fired the day I started working there. He made a scene in the west lobby, accusing his coworkers of worshipping Shakespeare and the Folgers. He called the Folger Library a church for Shakespeare and accused everyone present of idolatry. He ranted that they were puppets of the three city states: the City of London, Vatican City, and Washington, DC. He said they were subordinate to the Crown and were not free. It was all very disturbing. Anyway, tonight that madman returned, armed with a semiautomatic handgun, apparently set on killing everyone there. Luckily he and the other guard killed each other before Moll could do real damage."

"What was the other guard's name?" Rupert asked.

"By the name plate on his shirt, Carew. Why?"

Whyte was visibly shaken. He looked as though he were about to weep. He struggled through his anguish and asked, "And the item?"

"I don't have it," she said. "He didn't have it on him."

Whyte sighed. "Of course. He hid it there in that fortress somewhere." He stared her in the eye and asked, "And the mourning rings?"

Kavitha retrieved from her bra the counterfeit mourning rings she'd received from Satō when she'd sold him Whyte's, rather Benjamin Johnson's, genuine mourning rings, essential to unlocking the secret compartment of the 16th Century jewelry box. She placed them in the palm of Whyte's outstretched hand. He turned on an overheard light. Her heart raced as he brought his hand up closer to his face and examined them. Would he spot them as fakes?

After long moments, he finally tucked this rings into an inside pocket of his suit jacket, and turned off the overhead light.

"Carew was your back-up man, wasn't he?" Kavitha asked. He did not respond, so she continued. "By the look on your face you had feelings for him. You could have spared yourself heartache had you trusted me enough to get the job done. I *always* do."

Rupert Whyte snapped, "I will *not* be lectured by you, Dr. Netram!"

Kavitha Netram shrugged.

"What's Blalock's condition?" Rupert asked. "Will he live?"

"I believe so," Kavitha answered.

Whyte nodded. "Then you will continue to ingratiate yourself. Nurse him back to health; gain his trust. He wants to leave the employ of the Folger's now and ride off into the sunset, live happily ever after. Convince him to stay on the Folger payroll, somehow. And you keep working at the gift shop. I need you to stay in play at the Folger.

"Blalock got the item out of the vault, I'm sure of it. He's hidden it somewhere there in the library. We are going to need him to go back in and retrieve the item."

Netram nodded and said, "Yes, sir."

She opened the door, climbed out of the limo, and swung the door closed.

Whyte turned on the overhead light, retrieved the mourning rings from the inside pocket of his suit jacket and examined them until the tears welling in his eyes prevented him from doing so.

[0000]

Kavitha Netram looked down the street at the emergency vehicles parked in front of the Folger. She'd have to come back later to get Norman's Jaguar parked in Puck Circle. She needed to kill some time. A good stiff drink is what she needed, so she strode away from Whyte's limo, up 3rd Street, S.E., toward Pennsylvania Avenue, where the restaurants and bars are. The first bar she saw would do.

She was in a tight spot now, but she could still pull this off. When the coast was clear, she'd drive Norman's car back to his house, and move in. She'd take care of his Great Dane, Bruno, and his house. Nice touch. She'd visit him in the hospital daily. Stay for hours. Nurse him back to health, earn his trust. Live with him; share his life with him, until this job was done.

But why was she feeling so uneasy? Maybe because she'd gotten spooked tonight: that broken piece of glass in the door of the Registrar's Office, a perfect cut out of one of the hexagonal designs that adorned it. It had drawn her attention to the Reading Room, where Norman lay dying of a heart attack…as though on purpose; like someone wanted Norman to live.

On Pennsylvania Avenue, SE, she strode to the local dive bar *Tune Inn* and ducked inside.

[0000]

TRUMP INTERNATIONAL HOTEL
1100 PENNSYLVANIA AVENUE, N.W.
ROOM 1212
WASHINGTON, D.C.

October 31ˢᵗ, 11:51 P.M.

Bo Satō hurriedly unlocked the door, entered his room, and rushed to the guest floor safe in the closet. He took a piece of paper from his shirt pocket and, referring to it, keyed in the safe combination. He hastily swung open the door, removed a 16th Century Cinquecento style jewelry box, reminiscent of a small scale Ark of the Covenant, and scurried to the bed. He placed it on the bed and went to work.

A product of extraordinary craftsmanship, it was constructed of bronze, gilt, and silver, with a wood base. The handle atop the casket was a golden bust of Shakespeare and the box was adorned with eight extremely detailed bronze figures of characters from the Bard's plays, and four different coats of arms rendered in gold and silver, one Shakespeare's family crest.

There were two other identical jewelry boxes in existence, decoys, but this was the genuine article. This one required three mourning rings to open the secret compartment, not just two.

A light sheen of perspiration on his face, Mr. Satō opened the jewelry box, removed two jewelry trays one after the other, and tilted the box over onto its back. On the bottom of the box, he worked sliding wood slats, like those of a Chinese puzzle box. Subsequently, he righted the box. He drew a switchblade from his suit jacket, flicked it open, and used it to lift the back edge of a false bottom and then with his fingers lifted it out to reveal three small cutouts of Shakespeare's profile at the bottom of the box, one on the left side, one on the right, and one in the center. Afterward, he removed three rings from a pocket of his suit jacket.

Mr. Satō removed from one suit jacket pocket the two mourning rings he'd just purchased from Kavitha Netram, and from another pocket, the mourning ring he'd possessed for some time. He fitted the Shakespeare cameo rings into the cutouts, and turned the right and left rings simultaneously, one clockwise, the other counterclockwise. The ring in the center he turned a half revolution to the right, and then a half revolution back to the left. Licking his dry lips, he reached under the box, slid out a small drawer and found…nothing.

"狗屎 !" he swore.

[0000]

TUNE INN BAR
CAPITOL HILL
WASHINGTON, D.C.

November 1ˢᵗ, 12:07 P.M.

As usual, Kavitha received unwanted attention from the dive bar's male customers. Sitting at the bar, she brushed off pick-up artists one-by-one. On her third drink, her cell phone rang. She pulled her phone from her purse and answered it.

"Hello," she said.

"We must talk, Ms. Netram. But not on the phone. Where can I meet you?"

"What do you want, Satō? Our business is finished."

"No, it is not. Where can we meet?"

"In front of Tune Inn, on the 300 hundred block of Pennsylvania Avenue, SE, as soon as you can get here. Call me when you arrive."

"I will see you there shortly."

Kavitha hung up and put away her cell phone. *Shit! Now what?*

She finished her drink and said, "Bartender. Another."

Kavitha checked her watch. Satō should be outside any time now. She mashed out her cigarette in the ashtray on the bar. She dug cash from her purse and tossed on the bar before she sashayed to the ladies room, all eyes on her.

She snorted a few lines of cocaine through a rolled twenty dollar bill and then checked herself in the mirror. She saw no sign of the hard life she'd lived since her benevolent benefactor Rupert Whyte had rescued her from the slums of Calcutta at the tender age of ten and taken her to London. She'd been a looker even then. She had been working for the "antiques dealer" ever since. He'd paid for the finest education and allowed her a luxurious lifestyle, trained her to be a master of deception and cultivated her into a valuable operative. He'd shown her the world as they'd pulled off jobs around the globe.

Jet-setting and hobnobbing with the rich was a long way from where she'd come, and she'd be damned if she'd ever fall back into the gutter. There was good money in her line of work and she wanted all the luxury her money could buy. She slowly shook her head and muttered, "No way."

Working for Rupert Whyte had been lucrative, but she was ready to break away, go out on her own, expand her clientele. Now she was being bogged down by the botched Folger caper. She prepared a couple more lines of coke and then quickly vacuumed them up her nostrils. She snorted hard and savored the narcotic as it drained down her throat.

When the initial rush subsided she stared at her lovely, bronze colored face in the wall mirror. The sixteen years that had passed since Rupert had saved her did not betray her beauty or hint at her nefarious past. Her face was a perfect mask.

Hiding behind her exotic beauty no one ever suspected she was the kind of deceitful woman who duped men and killed them for money.

She wondered how she would look if the evil inside manifested itself upon her face. *"Probably Picture of Dorian Gray ugly,"* she mused.

Including the District of Columbia assignment and local ventures in the United Kingdom, she'd worked more than a dozen and a half jobs for Whyte, spread out over the years, all over the world. Rome. Paris. Madrid. Istanbul. Venice. Vatican City. Prague. Tokyo. Dubai. Cairo. Athens. Budapest. Vienna. Oslo. Helsinki. Munich. Short and sweet well-paying jobs, honeypot scams to acquire highly sought after rare objects, followed by termination of the marks, Standard Operating Procedure. This easy money she earned allowed her to spend most of her time as she chose. It had been great, certainly, but it was time to kiss Rupert goodbye and move on. All that was left to do is get out from under this Norman Blalock mess. Unlike the other jobs, the District of Columbia gig would not be short or sweet, if Benjamin Johnson failed to eliminate Rupert Whyte.

Satō rang her phone. She answered, "I'll be right out." She put her cell phone and cocaine back in her purse, checked her nostrils, and then strode out of the ladies room, head held high.

Kavitha exited the bar. She saw a white limo with Satō's Aryan Weightlifter Chauffeur/Bodyguard behind the wheel. She stepped lively to the Lincoln, opened the door, and joined Satō in the back. The privacy partition between the driver and the passenger compartments was already raised.

"What is it?" Kavitha asked.

"I accessed the secret compartment of my jewelry box and it is empty."

"So? Our deal was for Whyte's two mourning rings. I kept my end of the deal."

"That is true. I want to make a new deal."

"Let's hear it," Kavitha said.

"The item must have been in the Folger vault," he said. "I want it and I will pay you handsomely for it."

Kavitha looked him in the eye and said, "I am not saying that I am in possession of it, mind you, but how much are we talking?"

"Five million," Satō said.

Kavitha said, "Pounds Sterling?"

"Certainly," said Satō.

She nodded and said, "I'll see what I can do. But you'll have to be patient. Our inside man suffered a heart attack."

"What?" Satō exclaimed.

"I was there when it happened. I searched him before the paramedics arrived and it wasn't on him. Provided he recovers, I will stick close to him and find out what he did with the item. Regardless, it will be a while before he can return to work and retrieve the item, wherever he hid it in the Folger Library, out of our reach."

"How long will we have to wait, do you estimate?"

"I don't know," she said and shrugged. "Three months?"

"You may already have made the same deal with Rupert Whyte, to stick close to that guard and get the item for him. How can I trust you?"

"Don't," she said. "All you have to do is pay me more than he offers and the item is yours."

Satō nodded. "Very well. I will be staying at Trump International, Room 1212."

Netram nodded. "Okay. As soon as I know the deal, I'll let you know, Bo. Now, have your driver drop me off at 2nd and East Capitol."

Satō engaged the intercom and told his chauffer where to go.

When the limo pulled to a stop on 2nd Street at East Capitol Street, SE, police vehicles were still parked in front of the Folger Shakespeare Library. Kavitha told Satō she'd be in touch. She then exited the vehicle, walked into Puck Circle, and unlocked and climbed behind the wheel of Norman Blalock's mint-condition 1968 Jaguar XJ6 Series 1 with customized license plates **PUCK**. She closed the door, started the engine, and drove a short distance up East Capitol to Norman's $1.9 million Victorian row house built circa 1926, located near historic Lincoln Park. She turned into the alley behind the house and used the remote control door opener for his garage. Kavitha parked and climbed out, retrieved Norman's walking stick from the backseat before closing the door after her, and used Norm's keys to let herself in to the house. She then keyed in the burglar alarm code on the alarm panel on the wall by the door. Norman's dog Bruno, a Great Dane/Black Labrador mix, was happy to see her. The huge animal stood on his hind-legs, put his arms around her neck, and hugged her. She hugged him back.

"Hello, Bruno. Good boy. Good boy. Let's get you something to eat."

Bruno jumped down and galloped to his food and water dishes. He sat pretty and looked back and forth from his dishes to her.

Kavitha smiled. Like his master, she had Bruno eating out of her hand.

[0000]

17

WASHINGTON HOSPITAL CENTER
WASHINGTON, D.C.

November 2nd, 1:43 A.M.

When Blalock regained consciousness, he was lying in bed...in a hospital room. Sensors to monitor his vital signs were taped to him...and an IV drip was going...and his right leg was in a cast, elevated above the bed in a sling. And then it came to him. He remembered how he'd ended up there and then began to wonder how long he'd been there.

On Halloween night, he'd heisted a priceless artifact from the vault of the Folger Shakespeare Library.

The job he'd been commissioned to pull off by Rupert Whyte was as follows:

For payment of three million dollars plus the historic artifact, Frederick Douglass's walking stick, he'd agreed to enter the Folger Library vault after hours via the emergency back entrance and retrieve from the hidden compartment of a new Folger acquisition, an ornate 16th Century Cinquecento style jewelry box "Shakespeare's BlackBerry."

In the 16th Century, no self-respecting Renaissance businessman would have been caught dead without a writing table, a notebook about the size of a BlackBerry, with pages covered in glue and gesso that could be written on with a metal stylus and then wiped clean with a sponge. Even Hamlet had a set. In the first act of the play, when the Danish prince learns of his father's horrible murder, the first thing he goes for are his writing tables. "My tables," Hamlet screams, "meet it is I set it down!" Ergo, writer William Powers has dubbed the writing table, "Hamlet's BlackBerry", and used the term for the title of his book.

Mr. Whyte had shown him how to access the secret compartment of the jewelry box, which to Blalock was reminiscent of a small scale Ark of the Covenant. It was an extraordinary piece of craftsmanship, a work of art.

After he'd heisted the dingus from the vault Blalock had hidden it on the premises when he'd discovered he'd been double-crossed. Afterward, perspiring and breathing heavily, he had entered the Gail Paster Reading Room and paused to look at the portraits of Henry Clay and Emily Folger, located under a replica of William Shakespeare's tomb and straddling the back wall with the columbarium niche containing the Folgers' urns, concealed behind an inscribed brass plaque.

Suddenly, his left arm went numb and he felt excruciating pain in his chest, as though his heart were being gripped in a vise. He took his radio from his Sam Browne belt, keyed it, but could not speak. He dropped his radio and collapsed to the carpeted floor.

Not now, Norman thought…

He'd been told by paramedics who responded to the library for his medical emergency that his coworkers had revived him with CPR and an AED. As he was carried out on a stretcher through the west lobby, he saw the bodies of disgruntled former employee James Moll and Sgt. Lew Carew, who at the behest of his boyfriend Rupert Whyte – the same man who had hired Blalock to steal the artifact from the Folger vault – had tried to take him out on Catwalk #1 and take possession of the artifact. Evidently, they had died by each other's hand in a shootout...

Ahead, there was still the problem of convincing Whyte…and Satō as well perhaps, that the jewelry box in the Folger vault had been empty, but at least Whyte's henchman/boyfriend Lew Carew was out of the way.

Blalock was too sleepy to worry about it now.

[0000]

FOLGER SHAKESPEARE LIBRARY
CAPITOL HILL
WASHINGTON, D.C

November 2nd, 1:47 A.M.

Chief of Folger Library Safety and Security Malcolm Leonard and his second-in-command Captain Nathan Rockford stood on the periphery, on the landing to the Great Hall, along with a homicide detective, out of the way of Metropolitan Police Department personnel processing the dreadful crime scene in the west lobby. The bodies of Sgt. Lou Carew and crazed gunman James Moll still lay where they'd fallen, their blood pooled beneath them.

"Jesus Christ," Chief Leonard muttered. "How much longer are they going to let them lie there?"

"The morgue wagon will be here shortly," Detective Jacob Holloway assured him. "Two of my colleagues have already made the death notifications to next-of-kin, our Public Information Officer briefed the news media, and the crime scene investigators are wrapping up. So, once the bodies are removed, everyone should be out of your hair soon."

Chief Leonard said, "Good. We've got to get this place cleaned up. We open for business at 8:30."

Detective Holloway nodded.

"Now, you say this James Moll character was mentally ill? He was let go after he lost it here at work last month?"

"That's right, detective," said Chief Leonard. "Right here in this lobby."

"And another guard had a heart attack because of all the excitement?" Detective Holloway asked.

"Not according to Officer Peterson's incident report," Captain Rockford said. "Officer Blalock had a heart attack *before* the shootout occurred."

Detective Holloway said, "Just a coincidence then. How's Officer Blalock doing?"

Chief Leonard said, "We don't know yet."

"I hope he recovers. Well, I've got everything I need. I'll be on my way."

Chief Leonard and Captain Rockford thanked the detective.

Detective Holloway said, "This could have been a lot worse, you know. Sgt. Carew is a hero."

[0000]

BLALOCK'S ROOM
WASHINGTON HOSPITAL CENTER

November 2nd, 11:43 A.M.

Just as Blalock came to again, a young Asian nurse entered his private room.

"Well, well," the nurse said, "look who's finally awake. What's your name?"

Blalock squinted at her and in a hoarse voice replied, "Norman. Blalock."

"Good," said the nurse. "You haven't had a stroke since last we talked. What's my name?"

"Annie. Yu," Blalock told her.

Nurse Yu nodded. "That's right." She picked up off a side table a white Styrofoam cup with a lid and a straw and put the straw between his lips. "Take a sip." She returned the cup to the table. "I'm going to get your doctor. I'll be right back."

The nurse left the room and returned shortly with a doctor who looked Middle-Eastern. He said his name was Dr.

21

Hussein and described the angioplasty procedure he'd performed on him, Norman's heart ailment, and the statistics for recovery and for extending life following a heart attack with proper care.

Dr. Hussein finished his spiel by saying, "You're a very lucky man, Mr. Blalock. You've been given a second chance. Don't waste it."

"I'll do my best, Doc," Norman pledged. "Can I still take Cialis?

"Absolutely not," said Dr. Hussein.

"Viagra?" said Norman.

Dr. Hussein said, "No."

"Levitra?" Norman said

Dr. Hussein shook his head and said, "Your heart is not healthy enough for sex."

Norman said, "Damn."

"For now, let's just concentrate on getting you well, Mr. Blalock."

"Thank you, doctor."

Dr. Hussein nodded and replied, "My pleasure, sir."

Kavitha Netram entered the room as Nurse Yu and Dr. Hussein were walking out. The doctor ogled her as best he could in the brief moment he had. He wished he had waited a few seconds before committing to leaving so he could have lingered and scrutinized the beauty properly. Indeed, she was worthy of a closer look.

Wearing a tight, form-fitting short black dress with spaghetti straps, black pumps, and those black silk stockings with the seams up the back she knew he liked, a black leather handbag thrown over one bare, golden shoulder, raven hair tossed over the other, she was a sight for sore eyes. She struck a pose and smirked, "You don't look bad for a dead man."

She meandered over to the bed and hopped onto it. Blalock bounced on the bed. His leg in the sling shook and swung side to side and he winced.

Kavitha shrugged, smiled and said in her lyrical British accent, "Sorry."

Blalock frowned at her.

"So," she said, "how do you feel?"

Blalock said, "Pretty good for a dead man."

Kavitha snickered and nodded. "You're lucky to be alive. You'd be dead if the Folgers had wanted it that way..."

Norman raised a hand and said, "Please."

"It's true you know. I'll tell you all about it one day."

"Okay, Junior."

"So, tell me, what's it like on the other side?"

"It's a secret," Norman said. "If I tell you, I'd have to kill you."

Kavitha giggled.

Norman looked at her for a time and then asked, "Where's your boss?"

"He's around," she said. "He has to close this deal before he goes anywhere."

"You here to close it for him, Junior?"

She shook her head. "He closes his own deals. I came to see you on my own."

As if on cue, Mr. Whyte entered the room. Speak of the devil and he shall appear.

Ever dapper, cane in hand, Rupert Whyte sauntered over to the bed.

"Well, how are you feeling today, Dr. Blalock?"

"Fine for a dead man," Blalock answered.

Whyte chuckled. "Yes. Well. Are you feeling well enough to discuss business?"

Blalock nodded. "Of course."

"Where is the BlackBerry?" Whyte asked.

Norman shrugged. "I don't know."

Whyte took a deep breath and then said, "You have five million dollars of our...of my money and that's the best you can come up with...?"

Norman argued, "I don't even know if it was in the box. I never saw it…"

"Please, Dr. Blalock!" Whyte yelled.

"I couldn't open it!" Blalock yelled. "When I removed the false bottom, there were cutouts for *three* mourning rings!"

Mr. Whyte was taken aback, was visibly shaken. "Three?"

"Yes," Blalock assured him. "Now, I don't know if the jewelry casket in the Folger vault is just another decoy or the real McCoy. All I know is there's a third mourning ring somewhere out there, and probably a third duplicate jewelry box identical to yours. Whatever the case may be, it's no longer possible to get at it in the Folger vault to find out, not now with the new security protocols in place. Besides, I'm retiring."

"A third ring," Whyte muttered. "Another decoy?"

After a time, Whyte composed himself and said, "There is still the matter of the five million. You transferred it from the numbered Swiss bank account in the same minute it was deposited…"

"Yeah," Blalock said, "and prevented you from withdrawing the money five minutes after you deposited it. I figured I'd better hang on to it for a while. To renegotiate my fee."

"Tell me," Whyte asked, "Why did you asked for more money when you had nothing to sell?"

Norman smirked. "I figured a man like you would cover his bets and have someone else on the inside other than me and his girl."

Before he continued, Norman noted that Kavitha looked genuinely surprised by the revelation that Whyte had hired another inside man.

Blalock looked Whyte directly in the eye and said, "I needed to buy some time to make it out of the building alive…"

"Just barely, it would seem," Whyte interjected. "What do you want?"

"One million," said Blalock. "An additional five hundred thousand dollars. For dying." He glanced at his IV and the electrode wires flowing from him and his elevated leg in a cast and added, "And for pain and suffering. And for having your boyfriend Carew try to kill me."

Whyte considered the price and agreed. "Very well. One million."

"Write down your account number and hand me your iPhone," Blalock said.

Whyte complied, using the back of a business card, and then handed the card and his iPhone to Blalock.

Norman typed on the iPhone's keypad and after a couple of minutes, handed back the card and the cell phone to Whyte. The Brit looked at the screen and was satisfied that four and a half million dollars had been deposited in his account. He then put away his cell phone and tucked the card into his shirt pocket.

Mr. Whyte twirled the cane. "I have no use for this. I still haven't acquired my Holy Grail, but I see no reason you shouldn't acquire yours."

Whyte handed Blalock the cane and said, "For services rendered."

Norman examined the cane and then whispered, "Frederick Douglass's walking stick."

He marveled at the cane with a white handle made of whalebone or ivory or something else exotic and expensive. Norman gripped the handle in one hand and the wooden cane in the other, pulled them slowly apart and revealed a sword. He smiled. He waved the rapier slowly in the air a few times and then sheathed it.

"Care to accompany me, my dear?" Whyte asked Kavitha. "I've got another job in Hamburg, something to pass the time while the search for the BlackBerry continues."

"No thanks, Rupert," she said. "I'll sit this one out."

"As you wish," Whyte said. "Until next time, Dr. Netram, Dr. Blalock."

Mr. Whyte exited the room.

"That was some bullshit," said Kavitha. "But that's okay, I like your style."

"What about the mourning rings?" Norman asked. "Did you give Satō the real ones and pass the fake ones to Whyte?"

"Of course, I switched the rings. That's why we don't have to worry about Rupert anymore. He's failed his boss Mr. Johnson too many times. And Rupert didn't know the difference between the real mourning rings and the replicas I gave him, but Mr. Johnson surely will. He'll believe Rupert ripped him off. And Johnson won't be happy Whyte gave you one million plus of his money for absolutely nothing in return. Oh, yeah, Rupert Whyte's days are numbered. Trust me."

Norman didn't trust her as far as he could throw her.

"That's good to know," he said.

"I had no idea he had someone else working inside," she said. "But we don't have to worry about his butt boy Carew either. James Moll took care of him..."

"I know," said Norman. "I saw the bodies when the paramedics wheeled me out."

Kavitha nodded. "So, that's that."

Norman said, "I also know you clipped the 2.5 mil Satō owed me..."

"Satō owed *us*," Kavitha corrected him. "Yes, I took it. I deposited our money in a separate account for safekeeping..."

"*Our* money, huh?"

Kavitha slowly nodded as her soul-piercing dark eyes looked deep inside him. She said, "Yes, *our* money. We're a team."

"We're a team?" Norman said.

Kavitha nodded slowly.

"You know," she said, "this could be the beginning of a beautiful friendship."

Norman smiled broadly.

"Oh," she said, "I picked up our Jag from Puck Circle. I've been thinking we should change the personalized tags to SPLENDA. Huh? What do you think?"

"Because I'm not a Sugar Daddy…"

"That's right, Splenda Daddy," she interrupted. "You're sweet, but not the real thing."

"How did you get my car?"

"I lifted your keys," she said. "Well, you were dead, you didn't need them anymore."

"Tisk-tisk," said Norman. "Stealing from the dead."

"Oh," said Kavitha, "I've straightened up the house and I've been feeding Bruno and walking him. He ran out of *Blue* dog food, so I bought a new bag, the Lamb and Wild Rice blend. He *loooves* it!"

Norman smirked. "Okay. Thanks."

She took the cane from him and laid it on the bed next to him. "I'll take this home for safekeeping. I'll bring it back when they release you."

"Okay," said Norman.

Kavitha got up, grabbed the bed's control pad and elevated the back of his bed to position him upright, and then positioned his tray in front of him. She sat back down on the bed, grabbed her handbag, fished out an electronic pad, and placed it on the tray between them. "Fancy a game of chess?"

"Sure," said Norman.

"I'm black," she announced.

"No," he disagreed, "*I'm* black."

Kavitha sucked her teeth and turned the electronic chessboard around so black was in front of Norman.

"You know, we should have played this game a long time ago," she said.

Norman looked her straight in the eye and said, "We've been playing this game since we met, Junior."

Kavitha smiled and nodded. She then looked at the chessboard and pondered her first move.

Norman said, "Hey, you haven't broken into my safe, have you?"

Kavitha sucked her teeth. "Of course not. Stealing from you would be stealing from myself. You know, I think it's time I retire too; crime has paid well enough. Oh, I know, let's open an antique store in Georgetown. We'll call it, *Things Remembered*. Oh, and we'll play Jazz in the store during business hours. We'll be partners, fifty/fifty."

Norman smiled. He didn't know what her angle was, but he didn't feel like trying to figure it out just then. Instead, he chose to live the lie for the time being. He decided to relax and enjoy the ride while it lasted. He shrugged and said, "Whatever works."

Blalock watched Kavitha, thinking as he marveled at her extraordinary physical beauty and tried to reconcile it with what, by his estimation, must be a rotten core.

O brave new world, that has such people in't.

Finally, Kavitha made her first move, King's Pawn D to D4. Norman suspected her next move would be King's Pawn E to E3. He mirrored her opening move.

"Before we get the business started," she continued, "We need a vacation in paradise. Someplace warm and tropical, so I can work on my tan. The weather in England is bloody awful and I've been stuck here in this near-winter climate when I could have been stretched out on the beach somewhere. Even Malibu or Palm Beach would do right now. They don't compare to the white sand beaches of Europe or Aruba, mind you, but they would suffice right now. And soon. Just look at my color…"

Norman started to interrupt her and quip that to look his best on the beach; he'd have to wear a three-piece suit. Instead, he let his Bacall prattle on while he became lost in thought.

Satō would be pissed when he discovered that his jewelry box was empty. He might even eventually put two and two together and suspect the truth and come looking for him…for the both of them. But they would just have to cross that bridge when they came to it.

Norman replayed in his mind what had transpired between the time Carew made him fall and break his ankle and when he'd entered the Gail Paster Reading Room through one of the glass and metal double-doors off of the Great Hall: Norman had crept into the Elizabethan Theatre during intermission and hid the writing table.

Should it become necessary for him to retrieve the writing table, he had hidden it where it was readily accessible to him and yet would never be noticed by anyone, not even members of the cleaning crew, and secured it there with two strips of duct tape…

Norman Blalock had been guarding Shakespeare for twenty-five years and he saw no reason to stop now.

[0000]

WASHINGTON HOSPITAL CENTER
PARKING LOT

November 2ⁿᵈ, 1:54 P.M.

Rupert Whyte's black limo was parked next to Blalock's Jaguar when Kavitha Netram walked up, Kane's walking stick in hand. Whyte lowered the rear passenger side window and told her, "Get in." She complied. The privacy partition was already up when she sat down.

"What do you think of his story?" he asked.

Kavitha shrugged. "It would explain why he didn't have it on him when he went down. But what do you think Mr. Johnson will think of Blalock's story? That's what I'd like to know."

Rupert nodded and said, "We shall see. I'll fly to London tonight and arrange a meeting to discuss with my employer our progress, or lack thereof. He will not be pleased, I don't mind telling you. Meanwhile, stay close to Blalock."

Kavitha nodded and said, "Certainly. Give my regards to Mr. Johnson."

She climbed out of the limo. Before she closed the door she said, "One other thing. I just finished playing chess with Norm. He beat me."

"He beat you?" Rupert gasped.

She nodded. "Three out of three."

"You're the best," he said. "*I* can't beat you."

"He's got a fine mind. His gambits are extraordinary. We must take care."

He nodded and said, "Duly noted. Stay on top of your game."

She smiled and said, "I will. You do the same."

Kavitha closed the door and walked to Blalock's Jaguar.

Rupert took the two mourning rings from his vest pocket and examined them, long after Kavitha had driven off.

[0000]

𝔚𝔥𝔶𝔱𝔢 𝔐𝔞𝔫𝔬𝔯
𝔒𝔵𝔣𝔬𝔯𝔡𝔰𝔥𝔦𝔯𝔢, 𝔈𝔫𝔤𝔩𝔞𝔫𝔡

November 4th, 6:43 A.M.

It had only taken Rupert Whyte's chauffer, Kruger, about fifteen minutes to drive the 13 kilometers or so from London Oxford Airport to his palatial residence, set on seven acres.

Primarily, Whyte owed his wealth and his prestige to his wife Mildred and her old money. Marrying the sole heir to the Glücksburg Dynasty had given him the class and the power he otherwise would not have. She having taken on his name, now he himself was practically royalty. It was a damn sight better than the attention he garnered as a professor at Oxford and far more rewarding than the anonymity of an MI6 officer. No, he much preferred being the Lord of the Manor. It suited him.

Kruger parked in front of the manor, got out, and opened the car door for his employer. Whyte stepped out.

"Bring in my luggage and then wash and fuel up the limo, Kruger. We'll be driving to London this afternoon. Around 12:30, I should think."

"Yes, sir."

Kruger removed Whyte's garment bag and suitcase from the boot and, on the heels of his master, carried the luggage to the front door.

Fitzsimmons the butler opened the door just as Whyte reached it. He walked past the butler, not bothering to acknowledge the manservant's greeting, "Welcome home, sir."

Whyte removed his coat and hat and handed them to Fitzsimmons. The butler stowed them in a cloak room of the immense foyer. Whyte walked on, Kruger still on his heels.

Fitzsimmons told Kruger, "I'll take those."

Kruger set down the luggage and left the house. Fitzsimmons closed the door after him, picked up his master's luggage, and made his way up the long, enormous staircase.

"Welcome home, sir," said Gretchen the downstairs maid. "Care for breakfast?"

"Just tea," he said.

Gretchen said, "Straight away, sir."

Whyte nodded, looking at the morning edition of the London Times. "Your mistress still asleep?"

"Who sleeps?" said Mildred.

Rupert turned and found his craggy, *Clairol Born Red*-headed wife planted at the foot of the staircase, her decrepit frame draped in her favorite white silk gown and

31

robe, perched upon her claws, which, mercifully, were hidden from sight inside of toes-in slippers, for a change. Blue veins spider-webbed her limpid, white flesh, which clustered at her temples, stretching to the receding hairline of the wispy hair atop her crown. Her nose was bulbous, blood-red freckles spattered across it's boney bridge. Even from one he stood, he spied the booger in the left nostril.

"You might have told me you were coming home," she said.

Gretchen retreated toward the kitchen and Rupert strolled over to *Lady Clairol*, as he was fond of calling the old battle axe behind her back.

Rupert ignored the booger in her big nose and pecked Mildred on the opposite cheek. It felt like sandpaper.

As he withdrew, he had to muster all of his strength to keep his face from not looking like he'd just sucked a lemon. Instead he smiled his most charming smile, looked her straight in the eye and lied, "I've missed you, my love."

"Have you?" said Mildred. "It doesn't seem so. You have not offered me more than cursory, vapid conversation for two months now, over the phone or in person. No, longer than that. You're barely here and when you are, it seems your heart isn't in it." Her aged visage cracked further as she teared up. Her shriveled lips quivered as she added, "And my God, Rupert, I can't remember the last time we made love."

"That's quite a greeting, my dear."

"It's the truth, Rupert. Surely you don't deny it."

"Of course I deny it, Mildred! You're so dramatic."

Rupert took the fragile mummy into his arms and gagged on the stench of decaying flesh drenched in Liniment. Fighting the urge to vomit all the while, he kissed her passionately, as he steeled himself against her foul breath, which stank like hot garbage, and her mouth, which tasted like cigarette ashes.

When he ended the long, awful kiss, he held her at arms-length. He looked lovingly into her cataracts and said with apparent sincerity, "You mean the world to me, Mildred. I've been busy lately, I know, but I have pressing business. Acquiring special-order items can prove to be time-consuming, yes, but ultimately it is rewarding. And I won't be busy for too much longer, I promise you. And then you and I will have all the time in the world. Tell you what, we'll spend time at the French Riviera when my work is done. We can stay for as long as you like."

Mildred giggled like a school and smiled. The sight of her yellow, buck teeth almost made Rupert wince. Instead he smiled back at her.

"Dry those tears," he said, wiping the moisture away from her leathery cheeks with his manicured hand. He put his around her boney right shoulder and said, "Come on, let's sit and talk." As they walked toward the dining table, he continued, "How are the children getting along?"

"Fine, dear. Junior is doing well at Cambridge, as you know, and Emily is now working for CERN."

"Home of the Large Hadron Collider," Rupert beamed. "Jolly good! I'm keen on the work done at the Conseil Européen pour la Recherche Nucléaire, you know. The experiments they are conducting there using those two particle accelerators are expanding mankind's knowledge of the universe exponentially. I am glad that our daughter is working there, making her mark, as it were. No doubt, she will help make history."

Mildred nodded and said. "Indubitably."

They sat down opposite each other at the dining room table, a silver tea service and fine china cups waiting for them, Gretchen standing by. She served them as soon as they took their seats.

"Anything else?" Gretchen asked.

Rupert waved her away saying, "That will be all."

Gretchen curtseyed and made her exit.

Rupert sipped his tea and then asked, "How are things going at the antique shop? Receipts up?"

"Didn't take you long to get around to the shop," Mildred said.

"You know it's the only thing I love besides you and the children. Second to you and the children, of course. A pale second at that." *Paler even than your translucent skin, my dear*, he mused.

Mildred lit a cigarette and blew smoke like a chimney. She glared at him and said, "You only love the shop because it cleans your dirty money. You can't tell me the last time you were there, I'll wager."

Rupert sipped his tea.

"You say you're on hiatus, but do you actually plan to return to teaching at Oxford, Rupert?"

"Of course, Mildred."

"Good. I much prefer it when you're handy. That is why I put Arthur in charge of the day-to-day operations of the antique shop, so I could live here and we could stay close."

"And a great decision that was, my love," Rupert lied.

The Crypt Keepers Grandmother looked longingly into Rupert's eyes and cooed, "I must say I enjoy our daily romps when you come home for lunch."

Rupert threw up in his mouth a little. He choked the bile back down, bared his teeth in a fake grin, and lied to his wife, "Heaven on Earth."

[0000]

Gardens of St. Mary Aldermanbury
London, England

November 4th, 8:00 P.M.

Destroyed by the Great fire of London in 1666, St. Mary Aldermanbury Church, which had stood since the 12th Century, was rebuilt in Portland stone by Sir Christopher

Wren, but was demolished again in 1940 by the Blitz, the sustained strategic bombing of Great Britain by Nazi Germany between 7 September 1940 and 10 May 1941. London was bombed by the Luftwaffe for 76 consecutive nights and more than one million London houses were destroyed or damaged, and more than 20,000 civilians lost their lives.

Buried in the remnants of its churchyard, in the twice scorched earth of this twice blighted hallowed ground, are the remains of Henry Condell and John Heminge, key figures in the production of the First Folio of *Mr. William Shakespeares Comedies, Histories, & Tragedies*, which was published in 1623. The two had been partners with the Bard in the Globe and Blackfriars theatres.

In the footprint of the church are bushes and trees and gardens. In one of the gardens, in the old graveyard of the church, there is a monument to Henry Condell and John Heminge, crowned with a bust of William Shakespeare.

Before the monument to Condell and Heminge, two well-dressed Englishmen. The hair of the older of the two, Mt. Johnson, was silver and Mr. Whyte's was graying at the temples. When they required confidential, face-to-face communications, this had been their clandestine rendezvous point for years.

Mr. Johnson glared at the bust of Shakespeare. He slammed a fist against his thigh and muttered, "Damn it all to hell! I have never heard of a third jewelry box!"

Whyte assured Johnson, "Our inside man claims the box in the Folger vault requires a third mourning ring to access its secret compartment, which indicates that there are two decoy jewelry boxes, not just one."

"If the item was not retrieved, why did you pay the guard all that money?" Mr. Johnson demanded.

"For his services," Whyte explained. "It wasn't his fault the item wasn't there. And you did agree to it."

Johnson nodded. "How do we proceed?"

"I have my people doing more research," Whyte said. "Perhaps we can come up with new leads."

Johnson sighed. "I don't mind telling you I no longer have faith in your abilities, Mr. Whyte. I no longer require your services, I am going to hire the work out elsewhere. Let me have the rings."

"Sorry you feel that way, Mr. Johnson," said Whyte.

Mr. Whyte reached into his coat pocket with a leather gloved hand and retrieved the two mourning rings. He handed them to Johnson. He weighed them in the palm of his gloved right hand and frowned. Johnson palmed the rings in his left gloved hand, removed the glove from his right hand with his teeth, and let the glove tangle from his mouth as he felt the rings with the fingers of his right hand. He snatched the gloves from his mouth with his left hand and proclaimed, "These are fake! What kind of a fool do you take me for?"

Whyte shrugged and said, "I don't know. How many kinds are there?"

"What are you up to?" Johnson asked. "Surely you don't think you can swindle me. I'm afraid I'll to have Afshar looked into this."

Suddenly Mr. Johnson did not look so well. In an instant, his face was sallow and coated with a light dew. He grimaced and clutched his chest with his left hand.

Whyte said, "There is a fast-attacking toxin I am fond of using, undetectable at autopsy. The official cause of your death with be cardiac arrest."

Eyes wide, Johnson looked at the mourning rings in his right and then glared at Whyte.

Whyte wiggled the fingers of his leather-gloved hands.

"Yes," Whyte said. "The rings are coated with that toxin."

"You bastard!" Johnson gasped as he staggered and then fell to one knee, a second wave of screaming chest pain overwhelming him.

"I knew you would call in Afshar and I can't have that. I'd end up dead. I'd rather I live and you die.

"You see, even if I had acquired the item, it would not be yours to possess. It was never going to play out that way. The plan was always that you die and I possess the writing table, because it is my destiny to expose the immortal imposter! I just needed your money and your resources to get my hands on it. It's simply that circumstances now demand that you die sooner rather than later.

"Five minutes after you're dead, I'll hurry to your chauffer, tell him that you've collapsed, and implore him to summon medical assistance. Before the ensuing commotion, I will disappear into the night."

Mr. Johnson collapsed onto his back. He continued to stare up at Mr. Whyte even after he was dead.

Mr. Whyte smirked. After a time he consulted his watch and then reached down and retrieved the fake mourning rings from Mr. Johnson's dead hand. He took a Ziploc sandwich bag from his coat pocket and placed them inside it. He then carefully rolled off each glove from its base, upward, removing them inside-out. He dropped the rolled up gloves inside the plastic bag, sealed it, and then returned the bag to his coat pocket.

Whyte replaced the leather glove securely onto Johnson's right hand and then ran from the cemetery. He was convincingly frantic when he alerted Johnson's chauffer about his employer's collapse.

As Johnson's chauffer leapt from the limo, cell phone in hand, and raced into the garden, Whyte turned and strolled up Love Lane toward his waiting limousine parked some distance away.

So much for Kavitha's plan to eliminate me, that treacherous whore! Whyte thought. *Or was it* their *plan?*

Was that black bastard Blalock in on it too? He'd find out in short order.

Whyte whistled while he walked.

[0000]

BLALOCK'S ROOM
WASHINGTON HOSPITAL CENTER

November 5th, 11:01 A.M.

Kavitha sat on Norm's bed, the chess board between them. As she spoke, he admired her exotic beauty, her Raven hair and smooth, golden skin; those piercing eyes; and her body-to-die-for showcased by her tight, white top and her black yoga pants, accented by thigh-high black boots.

She said, "Benjamin Johnson should be able to spot the fake mourning rings straight away when Rupert turns them over to him. And that will be the end of Rupert Whyte. Then we will be free."

"Sounds great," Norm said. He made his move and proclaimed, "Checkmate."

Kavitha Netram stared at the board.

"Not again!" Kavitha said. "I will defeat you yet!"

"You'll beat me when you know how I think," Norm said.

"So, you keeping winning because you know how I think, huh, Norman?"

Norman shrugged. "Another game?"

Kavitha looked at her wristwatch and said, "No. I have to go to work."

"Work?" said Norm.

"Yeah. I still work at the gift shop."

"Why? Planning another inside job, Kavitha?"

She laughed and said, "No. Not at the moment. I figured it would be better if I stayed on for a while rather than just disappear…"

"Under the circumstances, it would be understandable if you quit," Norman offered. "You did witness two people kill each other. No one would blame you if you never came back to the Folger Library."

Kavitha shrugged and said, "It gives me something to do besides taking care of your house and dog and visiting you in hospital."

A tall, dark, and handsome man wearing a black suit and a black fedora entered Norm's room. Kavitha figured that he and Norm must have the same tailor.

"Luther!" said Norman.

Luther nodded and said, "Hey, Norm." He eyeballed Kavitha. "Hello."

"Hello," said Kavitha.

"Luther, this is Kavitha. Kavitha, my cousin, Luther."

"Pleased to meet you, Luther."

"The pleasure is mine."

"You're getting around on them good I see," said Norman.

"Yeah, they are like part of me now," Kane said.

Kane noticed Kavitha's perplexity. He reached down and pulled up his left pant leg to reveal one of his Ottobock prosthetic legs, rapped on it with his knuckles. "Top of the line," he assured her. He dropped the left pant leg and pulled up the right and added, "Matching set."

Kavitha looked flabbergasted. She stood quickly and said, "Well, I'm off."

"You aren't leaving on my account, are you?" Luther asked.

"Certainly not," she said. She gave Norman a quick peck on his full lips. "See you later. Nice meeting you, Luther."

"Yes," Luther agreed.

Luther Kane watched Kavitha saunter out of the room and then turned back to his cousin. "Daaaamn! What's up with that, cuz? That your girl?"

Norman said, "Well, it's...complicated. Anyway, how are you man? How's the private eye business?"

"I'm good," said Luther. "Business is booming. Divorce work is my métier. No shortage of married people wanting to get the goods on their spouses. The work is unsavory, but it pays well. How about you, you old dog? You're the one laid up. Are you on your deathbed or are you faking to get attention from that gorgeous woman who just left?"

"I'm okay. I could use a cigarette, though."

Luther shook his head. "That's against the rules."

"When have rules mattered to you, Luther?"

"Sorry, Norm, can't do it. You're better off without 'em."

"Well then, how about a thick, juicy steak, medium-rare, with a baked potato smothered in butter?"

"Sorry, I left your plate in my other suit."

Norman laughed.

"How long you in for?" Luther asked.

"I get out next week. I just have to follow the prescribed diet and take more medicine. The cast comes off in about six weeks, then I have to rehab my ankle. No sweat."

"You about ready to hang up that job?"

"Not yet," Norman said. "I have a workman's comp claim in. Figured I'd take it easy for a while on someone else's dime."

"Workman's comp?" said Luther. "For a heart attack?"

Norman laughed and then said, "Kimberley Mauldin said the same thing when I called her."

"Who?"

"The head of Folger's Human Resources department. No, for the broken ankle. I slipped on something and fell down some stairs at work *before* I had the heart attack."

"Okay," Luther said, nodding. "Sounds good. "You deserve a break. Why retire when you don't have to?"

"Exactly," Norman agreed. "Plus I have Aflac. With that and the workman's comp checks, I'll clean up. And I won't have to use any of my leave. I am on admin leave."

"Getting paid for *not* working," Luther grinned. "Work the system, cuz, work it!"

"You know it."

"Say, where did you meet the babe?" Luther wanted to know.

"At work…" Norm told him.

"They got honeys like *that* running around in the Folger Library? No wonder you don't want to retire! I have *got* to come visit!"

Norman and Luther laughed.

"Not quite," Norman said. "There are some fine women working there, don't get me wrong. But Kavitha is special."

"I'll say," Luther said. "She got a sister?"

Norman said, "I don't know. If she does, she doesn't live in the area."

"That's too bad. Had many visitors?"

"Quite a few from work. Let's see…, Jamal Swayne, D'Vida Mack, Tony Ellison, Andre Myrick, Carl Witherspoon, Lari Lavigne, Andre Myrick, and Charles Crew."

"You're popular," Luther declared.

Norman shrugged. "It would seem so. Oh, and Claire Natkin from HR stopped by with my workman's compensation paperwork and waited for me to fill it out so she could take it back with her. She also brought those get well cards over there, signed by everybody who works at the library, looks like. And Chief Leonard even stopped by. He wanted to know if I was going to retire now. His face turned red when I told him I had put in a workman's comp claim for my broken ankle. Like I told Mauldin, I told him to confirm it with Officer Ann Swann. She saw me limping that night and I told her what happened.

"Chief Leonard would love to fire me since he failed to get me to retire, but he can't while I'm on workman's comp."

"He's got it in for you, huh?"

"Yes. He says it's because he thinks I'm too old for the job, but I think he just can't stand me. He can't bring new blood aboard so long as I'm still employed there. That's what eating him."

Luther said, "He's just gonna have to suck it up."

"Exactly," Norman agreed.

Luther said, "He's passed you over for promotion a couple of times, right? You should file an EEOC complaint against him, for discriminating against you because of your age."

"That's a great idea," said Norm.

"Any other visitors, Norm? How about Leah Rosa Hinton?"

Norman said, "No. We broke up."

Luther said, "I see. You upgraded. How about family? Your children visit you yet?"

Norman shook his head.

Luther sighed and said, "Your ex really did a number on their heads."

"It's all on me, Luther. I'm the one who messed things up."

"Whatever you say, cuz," Luther said. "Do you need anything, other than a cigarette or a steak?"

"No. Nothing comes to mind."

"I didn't think so. Looks to me like you got everything you need. You got your hands full with that tenderoni!"

Luther and Norman laughed.

When the laughter died, Norm frowned and said, "Come to think of it, there is something you can do for me. You still have contacts at Interpol?"

"Sure," said Luther.

"There are some people I'd like for you to check out."

"Who?"

"I'll write them down. Let me have your notebook and pen."

Luther removed his pen and notebook from his shirt pocket and handed them to Norman. After Norman finished writing in his notebook and returned it and his pen to him, Luther looked over the names his cousin had jotted down and then asked, "What's up?"

"I'll tell you later," said Norman. "After you've checked out those people."

[0000]

FOLGER SHAKESPEARE LIBRARY
CAPITOL HILL
WASHINGTON, D.C.

November 5th, 12:00 P.M.

Kavitha Netram sat at the cashier's desk of the gift shop, looking busy, but paying close attention to what was being said. She was actively eavesdropping on Chief Leonard, Captain Rockford, and Director of the Folger Mike Witmore, who were talking near the guard's desk in the west lobby, posted by Officer Andrea Byrd. Kavitha overheard every word:

DIRECTOR WITMORE

We have several condolence cards here for Mrs. Carew. I'll leave them here for everyone to sign. I'll have Yvonne Barton pick them up tomorrow morning and I'll deliver them personally tomorrow afternoon, along with the flowers Lari Lavigne ordered. We've also made arrangements for a memorial service next week, which his family has agreed to attend. It will be held at the Lutheran Church of the

Reformation across the street, and Reverend Wilker will preside, of course. Carew's funeral is scheduled for the following day, in Lynchburg, Virginia, so this will give us all a chance to show our respects, without having to close the library that day. We'd have to; *everybody* would be at the funeral to say goodbye.

CHIEF LEONARD
You're right there. Wouldn't miss it.

CAPTAIN ROCKFORD
Me either. Carew is a true American hero.

OFFICER BYRD
You ain't never lied. God bless him! He saved a lot of lives.

DIRECTOR WITMORE
Indeed. Malcom, our meeting scheduled for three is still on. We'll meet in my office. I want you there too, Rocky. The Voynich Manuscript will be in the next exhibit and there are security protocols we have to meet before Yale loans it to us.

CHIEF LEONARD
We'll see you then.

Leonard, Rockford, and Witmore dispersed, leaving Officer Byrd at her post.

Rupert Whyte would have loved to get his hands on the Voynich Manuscript, Kavitha knew. One particular obsessed, filthy rich buyer immediately came to mind. Pity. Poor Rupert. Benjamin Johnson had surely taken care of him by now. May he rest in peace.

[0000]

BLALOCK'S ROOM
WASHINGTON HOSPITAL CENTER

November 5th, 7:21 P.M.

Kavitha sat on Norm's bed, the chess board between them. In trouble once again, she made her move, d4 Bb6.

"It won't be long now," she declared. "I'll have you on the run soon."

Norman smirked. He made his move, fxg3 Ne3 0-1, and then said, "Checkmate."

"Damn!" she said. "How did I not see that coming? Damn! I will beat you yet. Another game?"

Norman shook his head and said, "No. How about a game of cards?"

"I don't have a deck," she said.

"Okay," he said. "Bring a deck tomorrow. I've got plenty of decks at home."

"Will do," she said.

"How was work?" he asked.

"Uneventful. Oh, there's going to be a memorial service for Carew at the Lutheran church across the street from the Folger, next week on the 13th. They think he's a hero, can you believe that?"

"Yes," said Norman. "That's the day I get out of this joint. We'll have to stop by, pay our final respects."

"Are you serious, Norm? He tried to kill you."

"Yeah, but it wasn't personal. Besides, if he hadn't stopped James Moll, I probably *would* be dead. You too, probably. And who knows how many others. That makes him a hero."

"You've got a point," she said.

"Maybe Rupert will stop by, too."

"Not likely, Norm. He must be dead by now."

[0000]

45

𝔖t 𝔓aul's ℭathedral
𝔏udgate ℌill
ℭity of 𝔏ondon

November 7th, 12:30 P.M.

Everybody who was anybody attended Benjamin Johnson's funeral. Statesmen. Captains of Industry. Royalty. The Filthy Rich. Members of the news media.

The service was held at St. Paul's Cathedral, its magnificent dome gracing the skyline. Built atop Ludgate Hill – traditionally said to have been the site of a Roman temple of the goddess Diana – the cathedral sets 17.6 metres above sea level. Closer our God to thee.

One of the most famous and most recognizable sights of London, the 17th Century church, which was designed in the English Baroque style by Sir Christopher Wren, was filled to capacity. Completed during Wren's lifetime of work to rebuild the city, the Cathedral Church of St Paul the Apostle was part of the major rebuilding programme in the city after the Great Fire of London. It was apropos that the larger-than-life Benjamin Johnson's funeral be held there, as the church is part of England's national identity, having risen from the ashes to stand as a symbol of the British Empire's resilience. No one had done more than Ben Johnson to defend the realm, as well as the faith, or proven to be more resilient. The Very Reverend David Ison eulogized him as such.

Lord and Lady Whyte sat in a front pew along with Johnson's family, next to his widow, who was forty years her late husband's junior. Mrs. Johnson did not shed a tear.

When the service ended, Mr. and Mrs. Whyte filed out of the cathedral first along with Johnson's family, the multitudes following.

46

A dark man with dark piercing eyes caught up with Rupert Whyte and took him by the arm. Rupert stopped and turned to face the man.

Whyte said, "Hello, Afshar."

"Rupert. Might I have a word with you?"

"Certainly. Go on, Mildred, I'll be right along."

They talked as the mourners walked by them.

"I understand you were with Mr. Johnson the night he...died."

"Yes, I was," said Whyte.

"Why did you leave?" Afshar Ansary asked.

"I maintain a low profile. You know that. I did what I could for him certainly, but I thought it best that I alert Benjamin's driver and have emergency medical services personnel come to his aid."

"I see," said the Iranian. "And what was the reason for your meeting at the Gardens of St. Mary Aldermanbury?"

Whyte said, "He and I kept our dealings confidential, as you know, old man. However, seeing as that makes no difference now, he wanted to commission me to obtain another priceless antiquity..."

"What, Rupert? What was it he wanted you to obtain?"

"Not that it's any of your business, but Benjamin wanted one of the eight missing Faberge eggs, lost since the Russian Revolution of 1917, specifically, the Alexander III Commemorative Imperial egg from 1909. He'd gotten a line on it from a source, wanted me follow up on it. Why do you ask?"

"Just curious," said Afshar.

"Just," said Whyte.

"And what was the last job you did for Mr. Johnson, may I ask?"

"Seems as though you're interrogating me, old chum," Whyte protested. "What's all this in aid of? You and I were his employees and now our employer is dead. May he rest in peace. What does the work I did for him matter to you? *I* certainly don't care about the work you did for him.."

"We both worked for him, it's true. But I took care of his dirty work, and you picked up trinkets for him."

."What's all this then?" said Rupert. "What's on your mind?"

Afshar Ansary looked Rupert Whyte straight in the eye and said, "I think you murdered him and I'm going to find out why. And then we'll talk again."

"Outrageous! The coroner ruled that Johnson died of cardiac arrest. And even if he were murdered, you're merely a killer-for-hire. Who'd hire you to do avenge him?"

"Nobody," said Afshar. "I'll do it pro bono."

Rupert looked him straight in the eye and said, "Don't waste your time, Afshar. Well, I must be off. Mildred is waiting for me. Goodbye."

Afshar Ansary nodded. He glared at Rupert Whyte as he walked away and disappeared into the crowd.

[0000]

BLALOCK'S ROOM
WASHINGTON HOSPITAL CENTER

November 8th, 2:30 P.M.

Private Eye Luther Kane was holding a stuffed manila folder when he strode into the room, directly to Norman Blalock's bedside.

"I looked into those people on that list you gave me and…shit," Kane said.

"Spill it," said Blalock.

Kane gushed, "Rupert Whyte served with the Royal Navy, retired with the rank of commander. After that seems he worked for MI6 for a while, you know, that James Bond shit. Married old money, made from the African slave trade and diamond mines. Snatched up the sole heir to the Glücksburg Dynasty, some ugly old hag..."

Blalock snickered.

"Seriously," Luther assured him. He flipped through the file and showed his cousin a photo of Mildred Whyte. Norman shuddered. Luther put the picture back inside the folder and continued, "So, marrying that hag made him some kind of noble lord or some such shit. But that ain't all, no. He deals in rare objects for special clients, operating like some kind of international jewel thief...when he's not working at his antique shop in London ...or teaching history and English at Oxford...or freelancing for MI6! Let me tell you something: I used to do black ops and merc work, but I don't hold a candle to this guy. I killed people sure, but as a warrior. This dude's a coldblooded killer! And word is he kills to get whatever he wants, whenever he wants."

Blalock reached out and said, "Let me see those files..."

Kane held onto the folder as he continued, "Whyte leaves behind a trail of bodies around the globe, most of them "heart attacks." Known to work with some unidentified exotic beauty who sounds an awful lot like that babe you had up in here. Uh huh. She's in these files, too. A true-life femme fatale, sounds like.

"And my God, the last name on the list, billionaire Benjamin Johnson. CEO of Omni Oil Consortium. Sat on the Board of Governors for the IMF..."

Norman interrupted, "The International Monetary Fund?"

"Not the Impossible Missions Force, that's for sure. Yes, the International Monetary Fund. And he worked for MI5 when he was young. Well, he's dead now. Uh huh. Keeled over in some park or something in London last week, supposed to have died from a heart attack, natural causes. The description of an as yet unidentified man who informed Johnson's chauffer that his boss had collapsed sounds an awful lot like Rupert Whyte. Spies got poisons that make it *look* like your ass had a normal heart attack, see what I'm saying? Tradecraft is what they call that. Whyte killed Johnson, I'll bet you. Poisoned him." Kane stabbed a finger at the manila folder in his hand and assured his cousin, "It's all in here."

"Hand it here, Luther!"

Luther handed the folder to Norman.

As Norman looked over the files, Luther snatched off his fedora, scratched the back of his head, and said, "Man, *what* you have gotten yourself mixed up in?"

Without looking up from the folder, Norman said, "It might be better if we talked later. Now that we know we're dealing with spies, we should watch what we say and mind where we say it. This room could be bugged. Tradecraft is what they call that."

"Shit!" Luther swore. "I should have considered that. Instead I ran off at the mouth. They could know what we know!"

"Let's hope not, Luther. All we can do is be careful from now on. When I get out of here, we'll find a safe place to talk. I'll fill you in. Until then, no calls to each other from our personal phones and no more talking anywhere that may be compromised, including my home. Pick us up some burners, plenty of them. Slip me mine down the road and we'll use only those cell phones when we must contact each other.

"And whenever Kavitha's around, don't talk to me straight. Don't offer any information you think I should know and she shouldn't. Just follow my lead when we're talking and save what you need to tell me for when we're talking one-on-one. Got it?"

Luther Kane nodded and said, "Got it. I'm working for you now, I guess."

"You *are* working for me now. Wait until I'm finished looking over these files and then take them with you, lock them in your safe.

'I'm going to need for you to put a couple of your operatives on Kavitha and I, follow us. Follow the people following us, that is.

"Do you know anybody with NSA?"

Luther said, "Sure do. Good buddy of mine from my JSOC unit, The Mechanics works there."

"What is JSOC?" Norman wanted to know.

Luther told him, "JSOC is the Joint Special Operations Command. Operates out of Pope Field, Fort Bragg, North Carolina. We worked black ops worldwide, teamed up with special ops units from other nations".

"SEAL Team Six shit, huh? Why was your unit called The Mechanics?"

Luther grinned and said, "Because we fixed shit."

Norman chuckled and nodded. "Okay. Have your people photograph whomever follows us, get good headshots, and have your buddy at NSA run them through facial recognition software, see if he can identify them. I need to know the players and who is on the board."

Luther nodded.

[0000]

Grand Towers Hotel
Abuja
Federal Capital City
Federal Republic of Nigeria

November 9th, 11:30 A.M

Perched atop the high-rise hotel, his impressive weapon resting on its bipod on the edge of the roof, Afshar Ansary adjusted the BORS sniper computer scope of his QDL sound suppressor equipt M107 Barrett .50 Calibre rifle. He sharpened the image of his target, James Obano, who was roughly 2.4 kilometres down range, visiting his kept mistress at the Sigma Apartments, located on Embu Street. The

Barrett Optical Ranging System (BORS) has one hundred ballistic calculators built in for all available ammo, eliminating the need for a spotter. It instantly calculates the distance to target, elevation, air temperature, and air density. Today Afshar was using standard ball, 660 grain ammunition.

Obano and his men had been giving the corporation real grief for over a year now, operating in the Niger Delta, some 672 kilometres from Abuja. Known as the Niger Delta Avengers, the band of pirates had been costing Omni millions by sabotaging the infrastructure of oil refineries, kidnapping corporate executives, and raiding supplies. Management had come up with a solution to this problem and had called Afshar. Armed with all the necessary intel on the target and the right tools for the job, the operation would be a snap. In fact, other operatives were carrying out hits of other troublemakers in the Niger Delta right now.

Afshar had observed James Obano pull his shiny, black Mercedes into the parking lot of the Sigma apartment complex, park, climb out of the vehicle, and stretch.

Obano was dressed in a lime green suit, sweated out at the armpits. This clown reminded Afshar of the *Congo Dandies*, all dressed up with nowhere to go, strutting around in squalor. Afshar had seen the Dandies last year when he'd pulled off a job in the Congo. When he returned home from that mission, he'd looked up the Congo Dandies via the Internet and learned that it is a club, with traditions that reach back to the time of French Colonialism in the Congo. Amazing. Ludicrous, but amazing, nonetheless. Just like Obano.

Afshar adjusted the rifle stock to his shoulder and focused on his target. He lined Obano's head in the center of the crosshairs of his telescopic sight. He held his breath and squeezed the trigger.

His right shoulder absorbed the powerful recoil of the weapon when it's stock bucked once. Travelling at approximately three times the speed of sound, a moment later the round exploded Obano's head, like a watermelon dropped from a high place. The corpse dropped to the asphalt like a bag of cement.

Afshar quickly dismantled his rifle, put it back into its carrying case, and then slid the case into a duffel bag. He tossed the duffel bag over one shoulder and walked a short distance to a rooftop door. He sprinted down the stairs to the 12th floor, exited the stairwell, and stowed the duffel in the same janitor's closet he'd retrieved it from after he'd tampered with the hotels camera surveillance system, setting the camera feeds for the roof down to that floor on a prerecorded loop so he would not be seen. Whomever had left the rifle for him would retrieve it. He then proceeded to the bank of elevators and pressed the call button. Momentarily, an elevator arrived and he pressed the button for the 9th Floor, where he'd booked a room. The doors closed and he checked his watch: plenty of time to get his things and make his flight out of Nnamdi Azikiwe International Airport. And then on to Washington, D.C.

He'd had his operatives tailing Rupert Whyte since he'd left the United Kingdom, and where Rupert went, he would follow.

[0000]

WASHINGTON HOSPITAL CENTER
WASHINGTON, D.C.

November 13th, 11:05 A.M.

Kavitha, dressed in a form-fitting little black dress, pushed Norman's wheelchair to the Hospital Center Drive exit, Nurse Yu on her heels. Norm, dressed in a brown fedora, button-down tan shirt, brown tie, overcoat, and khakis with the right pants leg cut up the seams to below the knee to accommodate his cast, stood up. Nurse Yu handed him his crutches and he positioned them in his armpits.

"Do it like we practiced and you'll be fine," said Nurse Yu. "And make sure you take all medications as prescribed and stick to the heart-healthy diet we gave you."

Kavitha held up a thick manila envelope and said, "Got it right here."

"Great," said Norm. "More hospital food."

Nurse Yu said, "Take care, Mr. Blalock. See you back here next week."

"Next week?" Norm said.

"You have an appointment with the cardiologist," said Nurse Yu.

Kavitha held up the thick manila envelope and said, "It's all in here."

Norman told Nurse Yu, "Okay. See you next week then. Later."

Kavitha said, "I'll pull the car out front. Won't take but a sec."

Norman nodded and watched her sprint through the automated glass doors, and away.

[0000]

LUTHERAN CHURCH OF THE REFORMATION
CAPITOL HILL
WASHINGTON, D.C.

November 13th, 11:57 A.M.

Kavitha had dropped Norman off in front of the church and then parked the car in Puck Circle across the street. He waited on his crutches for her to return and then they proceeded up the church steps together. She held his crutches while he held onto the handrail and hopped up the stairs and into the church. When he reached level surface, he took his crutches from Kavitha, positioned them in his armpits, and made his way down the aisle, in the receiving line for Carew's widow and immediate family, including his infant son Lou Jr., and five-year-old daughter Samantha, seated front row.

After Norman and Kavitha said their condolences to the bereaved, they made their way to the back of the church, stopping briefly here and there to quietly accept greetings from coworkers who were glad to see Norman back on his feet, and sat in the last row of pews.

Kavitha leaned in and whispered into Norman's left ear, "Did you know Carew was married...with children?"

Norman shook his head.

Kavitha nodded.

Folger Director Michael Witmore stepped to the pulpit and said, "We are gathered here today to honor our fallen comrade, Lou Carew, Sr., and to mourn his loss with his family.

"Not only did Sgt. Carew save countless lives, he protected priceless artifacts with his life. This institution owes him a debt of gratitude that can never be repaid. However, as a small token of our esteem, the Folger has set up college funds for his son, Lou Jr., and his daughter, Samantha."

Dr. Witmore spoke directly to Carew's family, then: "If you need anything, if there is anything we can do to help, please don't hesitate to let us know. You will always be a part of the Folger family."

Mike Witmore took his seat on the stage and Chief Malcolm Leonard took the pulpit. He spoke eloquently about his fallen officer for about twenty minutes. When he sat, Sgt. Carew's immediately supervisor, Lt. Hank McAllister, Commander of the Armed Response Team, took the pulpit and praised the hero for another twenty minutes.

All the while his colleagues eulogized him, the Carew women wept openly.

When Lt. McAllister sat down, Reverend Michael Wilker stood and stepped to the pulpit. He said, "Welcome."

The congregation responded.

Reverend Wilker spoke directly to the Carew family in the front row: "I am sorry for your loss. I grieve with thee."

The reverend turned his attention back to the general congregation and continued, "I did not know Lou Carew, Sr., very well. Oh, I knew he was very friendly and helpful, based on my encounters with the young man, sure. But, I did not know him in life as I know him now; did not know that he was a hero."

Norman caught Kavitha looking at him, one of her eyebrows raised, and quickly turned his attention back to the pulpit.

Reverend Wilker said, "Lou Carew made the supreme sacrifice, gave his own life to save others. John 15: 13: *Greater love hath no man than this, that a man lay down his life for his friends.*"

The reverend looked down at the Carew family and told them, "Only God knows how many lives Lou saved that night by stopping that madman. He has indeed earned a place in heaven."

Reverend Wilker then addressed the entire congregation: "Let us pray."

When the congregation bowed their heads and closed their eyes, the reverend said, "Refresh the soul that has now departed with heavenly consolation and joy, and fulfill for it all the gracious promises which in Your holy Word You have made to those who believe in You. Grant to the body a soft and quiet rest in the earth till the Last Day, when You will reunite body and soul and lead them into glory, so that the entire person who served You here may be filled with heavenly joy there.

"Amen."

The congregation said, "Amen."

Just then a lovely young woman with a lovely voice stood on stage and, accompanied only by a keyboardist, sang solo as Carew's widow and family stood and slowly made their way up the aisle to the front doors, followed by Carew's friends and coworkers:

1 Amazing grace (how sweet the sound)
that saved a wretch like me!
I once was lost, but now am found,
was blind, but now I see.

2 'Twas grace that taught my heart to fear,
and grace my fears relieved;
how precious did that grace appear
the hour I first believed!

3 Through many dangers, toils and snares
I have already come:
'tis grace has brought me safe thus far,
and grace will lead me home.

4 The Lord has promised good to me,
his word my hope secures;
he will my shield and portion be
as long as life endures.
5 Yes, when this flesh and heart shall fail,
and mortal life shall cease:
I shall possess, within the veil,
a life of joy and peace.

6 The earth shall soon dissolve like snow,
the sun forbear to shine;
but God, who called me here below,
will be forever mine.

Outside the church, Chief Malcolm Leonard interrupted a crowd of people gathered around Norman, expressing their pleasure that he was back on his feet.

"I need to talk to you for a second, Norm. Over here."

Norman told his coworkers, "Please excuse me."

He followed Chief Leonard a short distance up the block, away from the gathering.

Chief Leonard said, "You know, being on workman's comp won't save your job if your special police officer's license expires. You can't be employed as a guard at the Folger without a license, right?

"Yours expires January 31st. Make sure you get it renewed, or that EEOC complaint you filed against me isn't going to save you."

Chief Leonard shrugged.

"That's all," Chief Leonard said. And then he turned his back and walked away, across the street toward the Theatre Entrance of the Folger.

Norman was pissed. He muttered, "Asshole."

Blalock returned to the gathering, talked with his coworkers a couple of minutes more, and then told Kavitha, "I'm ready to go home."

Kavitha nodded and said, "Wait here. I'll bring the car around."

When she was out of earshot, Donnell Curtis, the officer who had saved Norm's life with the AED, said, "What's up, Norm? Me and the fellows were wondering, is that you, man?"

"She's a friend of mine, Curtis."

Curtis smiled and said, "I see said the blind man. Okay, player."

"Knock it off, man," said Norman.

"Uh huh. Oh. She's driving your car, too!"

Norman smirked.

Kavitha pulled to the curb in front of Norman, got out, and opened the passenger door for him.

"See y'all later," said Curtis.

"Later," said Norman. He shook Donnell's hand and said, "Thanks for raising me from the dead."

"See you later, Donnell," said Kavitha.

Curtis smiled and waved. "Later."

Kavitha took Norm's crutches and he climbed into the Jag. Afterward, she closed his door and returned to the driver's side.

She put his crutches on the back seat, climbed in, and pulled off.

Donnell Curtis smiled after them and said, "Player, player."

Kavitha drove up East Capitol Street. Without taking her eyes off the roadway, she asked, "That was a nice memorial service, huh?"

"The best," said Norman.

"Really? I haven't attended many. Just this one actually. I'll take your word for it."

"Really? Well, I guess you'll just have to trust me."

Kavitha said, "Oh, I do. Completely." After a pause she asked, "Do you trust me?"

Norman answered, "I don't have to trust you. I *know* you."

Kavitha did a quick double-take and asked, "What's that supposed to mean?"

"Just what I said."

"Okay. We'll leave it at that…for now. Tell me, what did the chief want?"

"He just wanted me to know that he can still fire me, even when I'm on workman's comp, if I don't renew my license."

"What a wanker! When does it expire?"

"January 31st."

"Well, you have time. *If* you want to renew your license, that is."

Norman looked at her.

She asked, "What does renewal entail?"

Norman said, "I have to take a drug test, have some affidavits notarized, fill out some forms online for Pearson Vue and pay $84, and then submit in person the affidavits and drug test results to the Metropolitan Police Department's Security Officers Management Branch located in the Reeves Center, which is a pain in the ass. I then have to pay a $35 fee for fingerprinting."

"Who or what is Pearson Vue?"

"A while back, the city cut a deal to have the Reeves Center torn down and replaced with a new building in exchange for allowing developers to build D.C. United's new soccer stadium at Buzzard Point, across the street from Nats Park. Pearson Vue, a Maryland-based company, was supposed to take up the duties of the Security Officers Management Branch until it could move into its new digs in the new building. Well, the new stadium deal was approved without having to construct the new Reeves Center. The Security Officers Management Branch stays where it is, but we still have to pay license fees to Pearson Vue."

"That doesn't make any sense, Norm."

"Tell me about it. It's government officials like that who have turned Capitol Hill into Moron Mountain."

"Why is it such a pain in the ass to go to the Reeves Center?"

Norm said, "The Security Officers Management Branch is open Monday – Thursday. It can only process licenses for eighty-eight special police officers/security officers per day. The customers start forming a line outside the building around 3:00 A.M. to make sure they can get a slot when the building opens at 6:30 A.M. In the old days, we signed in and each got a number and then went to a waiting room until the office we had to go to opened at 7:30. Now the waiting room is gone. They turned it into office space for another agency. So, once you sign in and get your number, you have to leave the building and then come back at 7:30."

She whistled and said, "Wow. I see what you mean. And you have to do this every year? In the dead of winter?"

"That's right," Norman said. "And this time, I'd probably have to do it on crutches."

"Well, your cast should be off before the dead. If you want to renew, that is."

Norman looked at her.

Kavitha pulled into the alley behind Norman's house on East Capitol Street. He opened the glovebox and used the remote control to open the garage door, while she positioned the car, and then backed in. Afterward, he used the remote to close the garage door.

She climbed out, retrieved his crutches and the manila envelope Nurse Yu had given him from the backseat, and closed her door. She walked around to the passenger side and handed him his crutches when he climbed out. He followed her to the door off the kitchen and after she unlocked and opened it, followed her inside.

Bruno stood on his hind legs and hugged Kavitha, apparently ignoring him.

"Hey, big boy," Kavitha cooed as she returned the huge dog's hug. "Who's a good boy?"

Finally, Bruno climbed down and looked up at him for a time. And then, to Norm's surprise, Bruno stood on his hind legs and hugged him too.

"Hey, Bruno," Norm said. "Good to see you."

Bruno jumped dog and ran to his food and water dishes. He sat pretty and stared at them.

"That's the first time he hugged me," said Norm.

"No. Really?"

"I told you, he's my father's dog."

Kavitha shrugged.

"Well, I'll feed him and then I'll feed you," she told Norman. "I've been grocery shopping, so I can fix you heart-smart meals."

Norman smirked and said. "Great. More hospital food."

"Take a load off, Norm. Make yourself at home."

Norman made his way to the dining room table and dismounted from his crutches. He pulled out a chair, took off his overcoat and tossed it onto the chair. He put his fedora on the tabletop, pulled out the chair at the head of the table, and flopped down on it.

Kavitha took off her coat and draped it on the back of a chair. She filled Bruno's food and water dishes and then went to the refrigerator while the dog chowed down. She removed a pack of fresh chicken parts, placed it on the counter, and then removed pots from a cabinet.

"What are you going to prepare?" he asked.

"Boiled chicken with steamed broccoli and cauliflower."

"With zero seasonings, right?"

"No. You get to have *Mrs. Dash.*"

"Wonderful. I can't wait."

"I'll get the chicken started. Keep an eye on it while I take Bruno for a walk. I'll be back in 15 – 20 minutes. When the chicken's ready, I'll steam the veggies."

Norman nodded. And then he observed Bruno, now sitting pretty in front of the refrigerator, looking back and forth from the refrigerator to Kavitha.

"What's up with him?" Norman asked.

Kavitha said, "Oh, he just wants some soy milk."

"Soy milk!" Norman exclaimed.

Kavitha opened the refrigerator, grabbed a carton of *Silk* and poured Bruno a dishful, and then put the carton away.

As Bruno lapped it up, tail wagging, she said, "Good boy, Bruno. Good boys get *Silk.*"

"Oh, damn. I already have to buy that expensive Blue dog food for him because of his allergies, and now I have to pay for pricey *Silk* soy milk for his big ass, too. I don't even drink soy milk! He's eating better than me, living high on the hog, as they say.

"How do you know it's not going to give him the runs?"

She shrugged and said, "It hasn't so far."

"How long has this been going on...behind my back?"

Kavitha said, "Hmmm. Since the day after I started living here, after you died."

Norman ordered, "Well, don't give him anything else new until you check with me first. Shit. Spoiling my dog; turning him into an aristocrat. I don't want to come home one day and see him wearing a monocle and an ascot, so check with me first. I don't need any more surprises. Or expenses."

Kavitha giggled, "Yes, sir."

She walked over to Norman, leaned in, looked him directly in the eye, and said, "Your dog. Not your father's dog. Sure, you got him for your father, but your father is gone now. Think of Bruno as your dog and you two will get along famously."

Kavitha kissed Norm and then straightened up. She nodded and reiterated, for emphasis, "Uh huh. *Your* dog."

Norman smiled, nodded, and then agreed, "My dog."

Sitting opposite him at the dining table, Kavitha asked, "How was it?"

Norman pushed away his empty plate and said, "Great for hospital food. Give me a cigarette."

Kavitha said, "I don't have any. You quit so I quit. You can't expect to rise from the dead again."

Norman shrugged and nodded.

She slid a saucer containing doses of his various medications across the table to him and said, "Take your medicine. I added a Vitamin D with Calcium tablet to your meds to help the bone heal faster."

While Norman did so, Kavitha cleared the table, rinsed off the plates and utensils, and placed them in the kitchen sink. "I'll wash these later."

"Fine," said Norman.

"How about a game of chess, Norm?"

"No. Get a deck of cards out of that drawer right there. On your left."

Kavitha complied, return to the table, and sat down.

"Poker?" she said.

"Poker isn't that great with just two players. Ever heard of Tonk?"

"No," she said.

"Hand me the cards. I'll teach you."

He removed the deck from the pack, shuffled the cards like a Riverboat gambler, and then placed the deck on the table. "Cut," he said. After she cut the cards, he reassembled the deck and said, "I started playing this game when I was in elementary school...

"So this is an olllld game," Kavitha interrupted.

Norman smirked and agreed, "Not as old as Chess, but yes, Junior, pretty old.

"Anyway, many variations in play are possible, but generally, Tonk or Tunk, is a matching card game that combines features of knock rummy and conquian. It is played with a standard 52-card Anglo-American deck and is usually played for money, for an amount agreed upon by the players at the beginning of each game.

"Depending on the number of players, each player is dealt three, five, seven, or twelve cards, in turn. We will be playing with five cards."

Norman dealt the cards and explained and demonstrated as he went along:

"The dealer turns up the first of the un-dealt cards as the start of the discard pile. (Some people play that the dealer does not turn up the first card. The discard pile is started after the first player draws.) The remaining un-dealt cards are set face down in a stack next to the discard pile. These form the stock.

"Players total up the points in their hand. Face cards are worth ten points, while numbered cards are worth whatever they are, two, three, etc. If a player has 50 points (or 49 in some variations) he says, "tonk" and immediately wins a double stake from each player. If two players have 50 points the hand is a draw, and another hand is dealt. Some people play that a dealt hand of 11 or lower is also a tonk. In the case where two players are dealt tonk, then a 50 would beat a 49, 11 would beat 50, 10 would beat 11, 9 would beat 10, and so on. If no one tonks, play continues. The player to the left of the dealer begins, and play continues in turn.

"The goal of play is to get rid of one's cards by forming them into spreads. A spread is three or four identical cards regardless of suit (such as three 5's or four Queens), or three or more in a row of the same suit. A player may add cards to his own or another's spread. The winner is the first to get rid of all his cards, or the player with the fewest points when play is stopped.

"Play stops when a player gets rid of all his cards, if a player tonks and the opponent has equal amount, this leads the second player to win because it is called being "caught" or when a player drops, by laying his cards face up on the table. A player may drop at any point in the game (some play you can only drop before drawing), including right after the cards are dealt. When a player drops, all the players likewise lay their cards face up. The player with the fewest points in his hand is the winner. If the player who dropped does not have the fewest points, he must pay the stake to each player with fewer points. This is called being caught. In addition, each player pays the stake to the winner. If there is a tie, both players are paid. If the tie is between the player who dropped and another player, the one who dropped is considered caught and must pay double, with the other player being the sole winner.

"If the player does not drop, he must take a card from the top or one under from the discard pile or from the stock. The player may then lay face up any spreads, or add to any spreads on the table. If after this the player has no more cards, he says, "tonk" and wins. Each player pays him a double stake. Some play that a player must spread with six cards to tonk, otherwise the player goes out with zero effectively ending the game but only winning a single stake.

"If the player has one or more cards remaining, he must discard one card to the discard pile. If this is his last card, play ends. He is the winner, and each player pays him the stake. If the player has one or more cards left in his hand after discarding, his turn ends.

"If the stock runs out, play stops. The player with the fewest points in his hand wins, and is paid the stake by each player. If two or more players tie the hand is a draw, and another hand is dealt.

"Got it?"

Kavitha nodded and said, "Got it. Let's play."

They picked up their cards and examined them. Kavitha reached for the deck to draw a card, but Norman laid his hand down face up on the table – a Jack of Hearts, a Queen of Diamonds, a Ten of Diamonds, King of Clubs, and a Ten of Spades – and declared, "Tonk."

Kavitha smirked and glared at Norman.

Norman smiled.

Kavitha threw in her hand. Norman scooped up the deck, shuffled, and dealt again.

Kavitha won one game of Tonk out of seven.

"I'm done, Norm."

"Me too."

Norman put the deck back into the pack and stood. Kavitha handed him his crutches and they went into the living room. Norman removed the crutches from his armpits and flopped down on his brown leather sofa.

Kavitha said, "When are you going to play the piano for me?"

"I told you, I have to be in the mood."

"I've been asking you for a couple of months now, Norman. It's a shame to let this beautiful Steinway go to waste. Can you really play?"

"Wait and see," said Norman.

"Guess I'll have to," she said.

Kavitha perused books on his bookshelves.

"You've read all of these, I suppose," she said.

"Sure," he said.

"Really?" she asked.

"Pick one," he said.

Kavitha took a book from one of the shelves and said, "*Elizabethan Essays* by T.S. Elliot."

Norman said, "Pick a page."

Kavitha smirked, opened the book, and said, "Page 21."

Norman said, "'Christopher Marlowe.

"'Swinburne observes of Marlowe that 'the father of English tragedy and the creator of English blank verse was therefore also the teacher and the guide of Shakespeare'. In this sentence there are two misleading assumptions and two misleading conclusions. Kyd has as good a title to the first honour as Marlowe; Surrey has a better title to the second; and Shakespeare was not taught or guided by one of his predecessors or contemporaries alone.'"

"That's word for word!"

"Pick another book," said Norm.

She put *Elizabethan Essays* back on the shelf, grabbed another book from another shelf, and said, "*The*

67

Collected Stories of Chester Himes." She shuffled through it, stopped, and said, "Page 73."

Norman said, "'*Heaven Has Changed.*

"'A Negro soldier heard the order to charge   and with his company hurled himself   against the enemy and was shot and killed. The next thing he knew he was in a hot, fertile country, walking down a dusty road between two fields of blossoming cotton stretching to the horizons.

"'He walked and wiped his brow and looked from side to side and saw thousands of Negro men, women, and children picking cotton and singing a spiritual. They sang loudly and defiantly and even a little rebelliously.'"

She grabbed another book, leafed through it, and stopped. "*Renaissance Papers 2009*, page 75."

Norman said, "'*This Senior-Junior, Giant-Dwarf Dan Cupid: Generations of Eros in Shakespeare's Love's Labour's Lost* by Ruth Stevenson.

"'In spite of Archibald MacLeish's dictum that 'A poem should not mean / But be,' the readers of Shakespeare's poem-plays do expect to understand what is, in fact, going on in a given text, 'to know,' as the King says, 'what else we should not know.'"

Kavitha gasped, "You have eidetic memory. No wonder you talk about history as though you lived it."

Norman stared at her and said, "No one knows except you and me. Let's keep it that way, shall we?"

"Of course," Kavitha agreed.

They were binge watching *Oliver Stone's Untold History of the United States* on Netflix when Kavitha said, "Norm, I've been holding off asking you this but…did you…experience anything when you died?"

"Huh?" said Norm.

"You know. Did you get a glimpse of what lies on the other side. Is there an afterlife?"

Norm picked up the remote and muted the TV before he responded.

"Have you seen the movie, *The Return of the Living Dead*?"

Kavitha said, "No."

"Doesn't matter. It would have saved a little time if I didn't have to explain this, but one of the zombies, a half-corpse with its bare spine column twisting freely, laments, 'It hurts to be dead.' Well, I find the opposite too be true: It hurts to be alive.

"I didn't see anything 'on the other side,' but I *felt*... I felt...at peace. More peaceful, more...content than I have ever felt in my life. Don't get me wrong, it's not that I'd rather be dead. I just want to experience that contentment, that peace of mind before my life is over.

"When I had my heart attack, something Horace Mann said came to mind..."

"Who is Horace Mann?"

"He was an American educator in the 19th Century, an advocate for universal public education. Anyway, he said, 'Be ashamed to die until you have won some victory for humanity.' Well, as I lay dying on the Reading Room floor, I was ashamed. I've won no victories for humanity. I have done nothing with my life."

"That's not true, Norm. You've..."

"I'm tired," Norm interrupted. "Think I'll call it a night."

"Okay," Kavitha said. "C'mon, let's go to bed."

Norman turned off the television and Kavitha helped him to his feet and up the stairs to his bedroom.

She wanted to stay, but Norman told her he'd prefer it if she slept in the guest room. He told her where she could find fresh bedsheets in the linen closet down the hall and then bid her good night.

Bruno followed her out of Norm's room.

Norm stood at his dresser, staring at all the pill bottles on top of it.

He looked at himself in the mirror and wondered how much time he had left.

[0000]

CHINA DOLL GOURMET RESTAURANT & BAKERY
CHINATOWN
WASHINGTON, D.C.

November 13th, 9:57 P.M

Afshar Ansary sipped Oolong tea while one of his operatives, Danny Woo, gorged himself on Steamed Dumplings and Salt & Pepper Prawns with Wok Toasted Chili & Garlic.

Woo spoke with his mouth full.

"My people have been keeping tabs on Rupert Whyte. He's staying at his place on Linnean Avenue, but he has people following an Indian woman and a black guy." He pulled a flash drive from his right pant pocket and slid it across the table to Ansary. "Everything I've gathered on them so far – photos, names, addresses – is on this. I'll upload more data to you as it comes in, encrypted, of course.

"The bag at your feet under the table contains a basic field kit. Whatever else you need, let me know."

Woo downed the last of his tea and stood. Before he left he said, "Get the check."

[0000]

BLALOCK RESIDENCE
CAPITOL HILL

November 14th, 5:57 A.M.

Kavitha was wearing white wool socks and form-fitting black sweatpants and black sweatshirt as she did her stretching exercises while she listened to U2 on her iPod Docking Station with Speakers:

My hands are tied
My body bruised, she got me with
Nothing to win and nothing left to lose

And you give yourself away
And you give yourself away
And you give, and you give
And you give yourself away

With or without you
With or without you
I can't live, with or without you

She finished her stretching exercises and flopped down on the bed in the guest room. She pulled on black Ugg knee-high boots and zipped them closed, then hopped from the bed, grabbed her iPod from the Docking Station and her earbuds from atop the dresser, and then sprinted down the stairs, plugging the earbuds into the iPod and into her ears on the way. She clipped the iPod on her waistband after tucking it inside sweatpants, and opened the coat closet in the foyer. She pulled out her black North Face *Thermoball* jacket, put it on, and zipped it up to the neck. She snatched her black skullcap from the closet shelf, pulled it down onto her head, and closed the door.

Bruno came over to her and gave her the sad eyes.

"No, not today, Bruno. I'll take you for a walk when I get back."

The huge dog lowered his head and walked away.

She took her purse from the plant stand in the foyer, retrieved her keys, stuffed them deep into her right jacket pocket, and then tossed her purse back onto the table. She unlocked and opened the door and walked out, closing the door behind her.

The air was brisk and intoxicating. Kavitha breathed in deeply and exhaled several times before she sprinted down the front stairs and out of the yard, down East Capitol Street.

Bruno pressed his wet nose against the picture window and whined.

As soon as Norman looked out the front window and saw Kavitha running down the street, he rang Luther Kane's cell phone.

"Hush, Bruno! Hush!"

Kane said, "Open the door, I'm right out front."

Norman disconnected the call and opened the front door, positioning himself in the doorway to prevent Bruno's escape.

A small black vinyl bag in hand, Luther sprinted up the front stairs.

"Hey, Bruno," Kane said, reaching past his cousins legs to rub the big dog's head. Bruno wagged his tail so hard he almost knocked over the plant stand.

"Back up, Bruno!" Norman yelled.

Bruno sulked away, off toward the kitchen.

Luther said, "You're right. She jogs every morning at the same time, just like clockwork."

Norman rolled his eyes and said, "You don't know the half of it. She's got me taking my medication on time, and is scheduling all my doctor's appointments. She's serving up that hospital food breakfast, lunch and dinner. On time."

"Sounds indispensable," said Luther.

Norman continued, "She's got me doing twenty-five sit-ups, twenty-five chin-ups, and twenty-five leg lifts twice a day, morning and evening. And twenty minutes every morning on my recumbent exercise bike in the basement. She's like a polite, sexy D.I."

Luther snickered, "A gorgeous R. Lee Ermey, huh?"

Laughing, Norman agreed, "Exactly!"

Luther said, "Here are your burners, fool." He handed the bag to Norman. "I got us four each, and labeled them 1, 2, 3, and 4. We'll use our phones #1 a few times and then discard them and then go to our phones #2, and so on. I programmed the phone numbers into each. You are designated Romulus, and I'm Remus.

"I have a couple of operatives on you and Sexy Ermey: Baby Jane Watson and Richard Johnson. You know Dick, right?"

Norman nodded and said, "Yeah. Short guy, looks like Kevin Hart."

"That's him," said Luther. "Anyway, you and Kavitha are being tailed. Johnson and Watson got some good headshots and my buddy at NSA is going to run 'em through facial recognition software. He'll get back to me ASAP. Says he'll run all the photos I want."

Norman said, "Great. Keep me posted. Later."

"Later," Luther said.

Norman closed the door. Bruno rubbed his snout against Norm's left leg.

"What do you want?"

Bruno trotted to the kitchen. Norman followed.

Bruno looked at the refrigerator and back to Norman.

"Oh," said Norman. He went to the fridge, removed the carton of *Silk*. While pouring soy milk into Bruno's dish, he said, "Good boys get *Silk*."

Listening to the next song on her iPod playlist as she hit the road – *Goodbye Horses* by Q Lazzarus – Kavitha ran at a good, even pace. She took her usual route, from East Capitol and 9th Street, S.E., to East Capitol and 3rd Street, past the Folger Shakespeare Library, the Jefferson Building of the Library of Congress, the Supreme Court, and the U.S. Capitol, down to 3rd Street and Madison Drive, S.W., on the National Mall, and back to Norman's house via the same route. But today, she sensed that she was being followed, so when she reversed her course, Annie Lennox belting out *Walking on Broken Glass*, she decided to run up the Capitol steps and back down before resuming her return route.

Back at 2nd and East Capitol Streets, S.E., she removed her earbuds and ran up the front steps to the west side of the Folger Library and ducked inside.

Special Police Officer John Morris was at the front desk. He recognized her, of course, and had no problem with her story about needing to use the restroom before continuing her run. "I like the ladies room downstairs," she told him. "I'll leave through the back door when I'm done."

"Sure, you can exit through Door 21," Officer Morris said.

Kavitha ran downstairs to the basement, past the restrooms, and directly to Door 21. She opened the door and ran through the alley between the Folger Library and the John Adams Building of the Library of Congress. She dashed past the U.S. Capitol Police guard booth, where officers controlled access to the John Adams Building's parking lot and past 3rd Street, down A Street, S.E., which runs parallel to East Capitol Street. She ran past 4th Street, S.E., past 5th Street, past 6th Street, to 7th Street, where she turned left and ran back to East Capitol, where she turned right. That's where she saw the black limousine parked on East Capitol Street, S.E. And then its rear passenger window rolled down to reveal the face of a man she'd presumed was dead by now.

"Please join me, Dr. Netram," said Rupert Whyte.

He opened the door and Kavitha climbed in and sat opposite him.

A block away on East Capitol at 6th Street, N.E., Afshar Ansary sat behind the wheel of a parked gray Mazda 3 rental car and watched Kavitha climb into the back of Rupert Whyte's limo. His operatives had informed him where Rupert was staying and he had followed Whyte himself this morning, from Linnean Avenue, N.W., to here. Dr. Netram was Rupert's go-to girl, he knew, and he wondered what caper they were working now.

When Kavitha got into the car, the privacy partition between the chauffer and them was already drawn. Rupert closed the door behind her.

"Catch your breath," Rupert urged her. "Looks like you had a good run." When her breathing evened out, he continued, "Tell me, who did you sell the mourning rings to, and why?"

Kavitha sighed and then let it spill. She told him all about her deal with Bo Satō.

"It was a good plan," Rupert admitted. "Unfortunately...for *you*...your plan went topsy-turvy. But that's water under the bridge. No hard feelings.

"I want what I paid for, Kavitha. Get him back on his feet and back to work so he can retrieve what I paid for and give it to me!"

"Norman said the jewelry box was empty. Perhaps the item *was* in Satō's jewelry box..."

"Then why is Satō still in town?"

Kavitha and Rupert looked at each other for a time.

Rupert continued, "I think he's hanging around town because his jewelry box is empty. I think he cut the same deal with you that I did: Get Blalock back to work so he can retrieve the writing table. I was supposed to be dead by now after all . With me out of the picture, why not cut another multimillion-dollar deal, with Bo Satō. I'll have a talk with Satō and find out for sure.

"Is Blalock in on it?"

Kavitha shook her head.

Rupert nodded.

"I taught you well," he said. "At any rate, let bygones be bygones."

"Very well," said Kavitha. "I have a peace offering for you. In a couple of months, the Voynich Manuscript will be on display at the Folger. Von Essen will be ecstatic to learn that it is finally within his reach, I'm sure. Ecstatic and generous. Extremely generous."

Rupert smiled.

When Kavitha got back to the house, she yelled up the stairs, "Norman. Are you up?"

"I'm right here," he said.

She turned and found him standing in the kitchen doorway.

"Let me grab a quick shower and I'll fix breakfast."

Norman nodded and said, "Great. Hey, what was that song you were listening to before you went out for your run?"

"*With or Without You*. It's my favorite U2 song. Do you like it?"

Norm said, "Yeah. I've heard of them, but I haven't followed them."

"We'll have to do something about that, won't we?" She found the cut on her iPod and handed it to Norman. "Hope you don't mind using my earbuds. My ears are clean. I'll be back in a sec."

She sprinted up the stairs. Norm put in her earbuds and enjoyed the song:

> *See the stone set in your eyes*
> *See the thorn twist in your side*
> *I wait for you*

Sleight of hand and twist of fate
On a bed of nails she makes me wait
And I wait without you

With or without you
With or without you

Through the storm we reach the shore
You give it all but I want more
And I'm waiting for you...

[0000]

TRUMP INTERNATIONAL HOTEL
1100 PENNSYLVANIA AVENUE, N.W.
ROOM 1212
WASHINGTON, D.C.

November 14th, 7:57 P.M.

When Bo Satō came to, he was duct taped to a chair, and gagged. Rupert Whyte stood over him, a hypodermic syringe in hand.

Rupert said, "Hello, Bo."

Terror widened Satō's eyes.

Rupert referred to the chemical in the syringe, "This causes extreme discomfort without any physical damage whatsoever. It attacks the nervous system and makes one's skin feel as though it were on fire. The chemical in the other syringe there on the nightstand alleviates the pain instantly."

Rupert swabbed Bo's right arm and then injected the chemical into him. Immediately, Bo grimaced in pain, mumbled, and began to struggle against his restraints. Rupert looked at his watch.

'In five minutes," Rupert said, "which will seem like five hours to you, I will administer the antidote, and then we'll have a little talk, quietly, civilly. If I like what you tell me, that will be the end of it. If I don't….." He shrugged and continued, "It's up to you, old man."

Ten minutes later, Bo had told Rupert everything, even the combination to his hotel safe, where Rupert found Bo's jewelry box..

Still secured to the chair and now gagged once again, Bo stared at Rupert, waiting for whatever would come next.

Rupert said, "Those drugs will be out of your system in eight hours. Then I will administer an untraceable toxin that will simulate a heart attack. The local coroner will rule the cause and manner of your death as cardiac arrest, natural causes."

Bo Satō struggled against his restraints and protested as best he could with the gag in his mouth.

Rupert said, "Don't expect your muscular bodyguard to rescue you. He's fast asleep in his room and will be for approximately twelve hours. Room service didn't agree with him. He'll probably be the one who discovers your body, though." Rupert rubbed his hands together and said, "Let's see what's on the telly, shall we? It will help pass the time."

[0000]

TRUMP INTERNATIONAL HOTEL
1100 PENNSYLVANIA AVENUE, N.W.
ROOM 1010
WASHINGTON, D.C.

November 19th, 7:47 A.M.

Afshar Ansary stared at the screen of his laptop, studying the images of Whyte's D.C., people his operatives

78

had been tailing, as well as the intel his operatives had gathered on those individuals. Photos of Rupert meeting with Dr. Kavitha Netram; Netram with that black security guard Norman Blalock; Netram going to and leaving from work at the Folger Shakespeare Library, and to and from Blalock's residence.

He figured that Whyte must be using Blalock and Netram to acquire some priceless artifact from the library, and probably had killed Ben Johnson to cut him out in favor of another interested party. And Afshar was determined to discover what they were after and who had outbid Mr. Johnson to possess the item. And then he would make them pay.

[0000]

FOLGER SHAKESPEARE LIBRARY
CAPITOL HILL
WASHINGTON, D.C.

November 19th, 12:33 P.M.

Afshar Ansary entered the Folger Library through its Theatre Entrance. The Box Office was on his left, the Great Hall to his right, and the Folger Theatre directly in front of him. There was a large monitor mounted to the right of the theatre doors, from where he stood, cycling scenes of Folger life: ads for upcoming events, photos of the theatre, the Gail Paster Reading Room, the Great Hall, docents interacting with visitors, Shakespeare's Birthday activities in front of the library.

Afshar turned right, walked up three steps, and strolled through the Great Hall. He grabbed an exhibition guide from a stand on his right and perused the *500 Years of Oxford Treasures* exhibit, and also admired the exhibition hall's 30-foot-high plaster strapwork ceiling, adorned here and there with Shakespeare's coat of arms; Appalachian white oak paneling; and ornamental floor tiles.

He learned from the exhibition guide that *Corpus Christi College, founded 500 years ago in 1517, is one of the oldest of the 38 self-governing colleges at the modern University of Oxford, and is a repository of extraordinary treasures, few of which have ever been seen by the public. To mark its 500th anniversary, a selection of fifty manuscripts and early printed books from its celebrated Library, ranging in date from the 10th to the 17th centuries, is being brought to America for the first time.*

Focusing on the first hundred years of the College's existence, the exhibition introduces its Founder, Richard Fox, powerful Bishop of Winchester and adviser to Henry VII and Henry VIII, and its first President, John Claymond, who laid the foundations of the Library's great collection. From the start, Corpus—the first Renaissance college at Oxford— was to pursue Humanist ideals of scholarship in three languages: not just Latin, but also Greek and Hebrew, the original languages of the Bible, along with such other subjects as Astronomy, Mathematics, Medicine, and Philosophy.

A series of display-cases present books in each of these languages, including a number that are bilingual and even trilingual. Most notable among them are a group that has been called "the most important collection of Anglo-Jewish manuscripts in the world"; these works of the 12th and 13th centuries include a series of volumes apparently commissioned by Christians from Jews, from which to learn Hebrew and study biblical texts in their original language, as well as the commentaries of Rashi and what is thought to be the oldest surviving Ashkenazi prayer book.

Highlighting Corpus' role in the development of science and medicine at Oxford, the exhibition finishes with a series of ground-breaking works, from Galileo's first observation of the moon using a telescope and Sir Isaac

Newton's autograph observations of Halley's comet to Hooke's observations of insects using a microscope and Vesalius' studies of the human body.

On the west side of the Great Hall, he observed Rupert's go-to girl working at the Folger Gift Shop, waiting on an elderly gentleman.

He wondered why Dr. Kavitha Netram was working there, performing such menial tasks; what inside job she and her partners were scheming to pull off.

[0000]

GEORGETOWN
WASHINGTON, D.C.

December 14th, 12:53 P.M.

Norman leaned back on his crutches and looked over the front of the prime commercial property on M Street, N.W., bearing a **FOR LEASE** sign as Kavitha gushed about the place. She ended her spiel with, "It's a perfect location and the right price, Norman. You are looking at the future home of *Things Remembered Antique Shop!*"

Norm looked away from the building and turned his attention down the street. But as he spoke, he was looking further than that. Way back. Kavitha had seen that look in his eyes before.

Norman said, "Lots of history here. This area is where black people were concentrated in this city, from the late 19th to early 20th Century. They were laborers at the Foundry, the Washington Flour mill, a power generating plant for the old Capital Traction streetcar system, a lumber yard, a cement works, and a meat rendering plant. And yet they could only afford to live in poverty near where they labored, crammed on top of each other in so-called Alley Dwellings, deplorable, unsanitary rumbles unfit for

Americans to live in. Five to six thousand African Americans paid low rent housing in the alley dwellings. The government decided to eliminate 'Negro occupancy'.

"On June 12, 1934 the District of Columbia Alley Dwelling Act was passed, establishing the Washington Housing Authority as an independent agency. The government fought tirelessly to eliminate the alley dwelling lifestyle and to improve the situation which was the cause for the New Deal. The government tore down the hovels, cleared out the Negroes, and renovated the area. And that is a brief history of how Georgetown became prime real estate, and a fabulous place to live.

"Slavery didn't end in 1865. It just evolved."

Kavitha said playfully, "What better revenge then for one of you to return and open a business among the elite? Am I right? Django unchained."

Norman and Kavitha had a good laugh, right up until Rupert Whyte stepped up to them.

"Dr. Blalock, Dr. Netram," he said. "My, aren't we chipper. Care to share the joke?"

"Had to be there," said Norman. "Hello, Rupert."

Rupert nodded. He said, "Isn't it great, having the band back together again?"

"Sure," said Kavitha.

"Come," Rupert said, "let's sit down and have a chat. My limo is right this way."

Norman glared at Kavitha and then they followed Rupert.

Seated opposite Rupert in the back of the limo, Norman and Kavitha sat quietly and let him run the show.

Rupert said, "Let's not play games. I know you tried to have me killed. You wanted me out of the way to cut a deal of your own. Nothing personal, just business.

"I had a chat with Bo Satō and examined his jewelry box. His box was a decoy, too. The one in the Folger vault is the genuine article, and you have the writing table. It is hidden inside of the Folger and you are going to get it for me. Need I spell out why you are going to get it for me?"

Norman said, "No, that won't be necessary. You'll make me suffer if I don't."

Rupert shook his head slowly and grinned, "No. *Both* of you.

"All you had to do was honor our agreement and our business would have been over…"

Norman interrupted, "Yeah, and I'd be dead by now. The minute you'd gotten your hands on the BlackBerry I would have been taken out."

Rupert said, "You're being paranoid, Dr. Blalock. I'm a businessman, not a murderer. I offered you good money for your services. I have no reason to kill you…unless you try to screw me again!

"Now, to make amends for screwing me the first time, you're going to steal the Voynich Manuscript for me."

"How am I supposed to do that?" Norman said. "It's at Yale University's Beinecke Rare Book and Manuscript Library."

Rupert said, "It's going to be on loan to the Folger Library in a couple of months. You must return to work ASAP, case the job. I understand security is being enhanced just for the manuscript."

"How did you find out it was coming?" Norman asked.

Rupert looked at Kavitha and then back to Blalock. He said, "A little birdy told me."

Norman looked at Kavitha, but she would not make eye contact.

Rupert said, "But I want the writing table as soon as you return to work. First day."

Norman said, "How do you expect me to get away with stealing an item from a display case? As soon as they see the case is empty, the world will catch fire."

"My client has a counterfeit Voynich Manuscript, which I will give to you when the time is right. Substitute it for the real thing and no one will be the wiser. By the time anyone finds out, you'll be retired."

Norman nodded and said, "I see."

Whyte said, "That's all for now. Dismissed. Back to work, Norm, ASAP. And I reiterate, don't try to screw me again. You cannot outsmart me. You're out of your league, Dr. Blalock."

Norman opened the door and he and Kavitha climbed out of the black limo.

The half-hour-long drive home was quiet. Norman usually listened to music in the car, but he switched off the sound system when Kavitha switched on his Jag. And neither said a word. The story was different once Kavitha parked the car in the garage and they went into his house.

After hugs from Bruno, Norman turned to Kavitha and said, ""You think you can run a game on me? Let's open an antique shop, Norm. We're partners. You must think I'm Sammy Sausagehead!"

Kavitha said, "Norman..."

Norman continued, "You think I don't know why you've been hanging around? You think I believe you care about me?"

"I *do* care about you, Norm! He's got me under his thumb, too. For ten years now, ever since he pulled me from a gutter in Calcutta. I'm trying to be rid of him..."

"Then why did you bring him this new job, Kavitha? Now, I get you ingratiating yourself with me so you can get your hands on the dingus for your boss, that's understandable. What I don't get is why you brought this new job to Rupert Whyte if you're just working for him and aren't his partner?"

"We're under the gun here. I used the only bargaining chip I had to buy us some time. He means to kill the both of us once he has what he wants, no doubt about it. We have got to get out from under, *both* of us have got to get out from under.

"So, what you're saying is we're partners now that your head is on the chopping block too. Partners like we were with Bo Satō? Right? You tried to screw me on that deal, and probably will try to screw me on this one."

Kavitha shook her head.

"I've been trying for years to break out on my own and nobody's going to stand in my way now, Norman."

"Nobody wants to break out on their own more than me, baby. I've been guarding the Folger Library for decades when I should have been teaching. That's what I wanted out of life; it was my calling. I committed one stupid indiscretion and cheated myself out of being who I was supposed to be. Now all I want is to live on my own terms and I'm running out of time."

"We are who we are, Norm. But we *can* become who we want to be. It's never too late to do that. If we work together, we can win."

Kavitha threw her arms around his neck and kissed him passionately.

When his lips were free, Norman looked her in the eye and said, "Don't tell me you love me."

"What if I do?"

"I'd rather you like me."

"What's the difference?"

"Plenty. I love my children, but I don't like them. I'd kill for them, but we don't enjoy each other's company."

Kavitha said, "Good point." She kissed him passionately again, looked him in the eye, and said, "I like you."

"I like you, too," Norman said. 'Get out."

"What?"

"We're partners until we see this thing through to the end, but you can keep your bullshit. Pack your shit and get out."

"Who is going to take care of you?"

"Not your concern," said Norman.

Kavitha nodded and let him go.

He said, "One more thing: who is the buyer for the Voynich Manuscript?"

"Wolfgang Von Essen," she answered. "He's a billionaire collector. Rupert says Von Essen owns *the* Mona Lisa. The one hanging in the Louvre is counterfeit."

Norman said, "Damn."

Thirty minutes later, suitcase in hand, "Kavitha announced, "My Uber is here."

"See you later," Norman said.

As soon as she closed the door behind her, Norman pulled Burner #1 from his pants pocket and dialed Remus. He hopped to the picture window and watched her climb in back of a tan Toyota Camry.

Bruno watched Kavitha through the window, too. When the Camry pulled off, he threw back his head and howled.

"Hush!" said Norman. When his cousin answered the phone, he said, "I need for you to check out someone else for me. Wolfgang Von Essen."

"What's the matter with your dog?"

"Never mind him," said Norman. "Check out Wolfgang Von Essen."

Luther said, "Wait, let me grab a pad and pen. Okay, that's Wolf-gang…Von…Es…'sen' with an ' o' or an 'e'?"

"I don't know, Luther.. Run it both ways."

"Essen. Esson. German?"

"Sounds like, yeah. Germany is where *I'd* start looking."

"I'll let you know what I find as soon as I find it."

"Thanks, cuz. Catch you later."
Luther said, "Watch your six."
Norman disconnected the call.
"Bruno! Hush!"

[0000]

SUITE HOME DOWNTOWN DC APARTMENTS
300 MASSACHUSETTS AVENUE N.W.
WASHINGTON, D.C.

December 14th, 3:59 P.M.

Kavitha let herself in to her luxury furnished *Suite Home* apartment, which featured a full kitchen with dishwasher, a flat-screen TV with cable in the living room, and free Wi-Fi. She'd held on to the place as a base of operations while she'd continued to work the Folger job, which had run much longer than she'd anticipated, thanks to Norman. What the hell? She wasn't paying for the apartment, anyway.

Suite Home's clientele primarily are business travelers who prefer short-leasing an apartment to renting a hotel room when on assignment for two or three weeks or more. So far she'd been working this gig for close to three months.

Her place was nicely appointed and was within 1.9 kilometres of the White House, the National Mall, and the Smithsonian Institution. It was just a fifteen-minute walk away from the United States Capitol; just a ten-minute walk from Union Station; less than a ten-minute walk away from Rosa Mexicano restaurant; and just a five-minute walk away from her favorite, Graffiato restaurant.

In the bedroom, she threw her purse on top of the nightstand, threw her coat onto a chair, and flopped backwards onto the king size bed. She exhaled slowly.

Kavitha considered how good she had been treating Norman and Bruno. She hoped that she had become indispensable and soon would be back in the fold.

She could not do what must be done on her own and neither could he. Like it or not, they were partners.

Kavitha turned in early. She woke with a start at about 3:00 A.M. when the lamp on her nightstand was turned on and she found a man in her room.

"Relax," said the man as he sat down in a chair near her bed. "If I wanted you dead, you'd be dead already."

"Afshar Ansary?" she said.

He smiled and said, "You remember me. Excellent."

She sat up in bed and said, "What do you want?" .

He said, "I want to know what you and Rupert and that black man are up to at the Folger Library, and what it all has to do with Benjamin Johnson's death."

[0000]

BLALOCK RESIDENCE
CAPITOL HILL

December 15th, 6:57 A.M.

It had been quite a struggle to get dressed on his own, and make it down the stairs, and put on his hat and coat, and put on Bruno's leash, but the dog had to go for a walk. It was a task he'd never relished, even when he'd been able-bodied. It was job! He had to carry big pooper-scooper bags to handle his little pony's loads.

Norman could use only one crutch if he was to have any hope controlling the powerful, 150-pound beast, so he leaned one against the plant stand and adjusted the crutch in his right armpit.

"Okay, Bruno, behave now."

Norman unlocked the door and stepped outside with the behemoth. As he closed his front door, Bruno bolted. Norman twirled, and fell to his left knee, his crutch gone airborne. He lost his grip on the leash and the great creature was free.

"Bruno! Come back here!"

The brute never once looked back.

Norman last saw Bruno galloping out of his front yard, and down East Capitol Street.

"Son of a bitch!" he said.

As he struggled to his feet, Kavitha, suitcase in hand, entered the front yard, Bruno on her heels, his leash dragging on the ground behind him.

Norman said to Bruno, "C'mon. She doesn't even have to hold your leash, huh?"

Kavitha said, "I was on my way here in an Uber when I saw him running free. I had the driver let me out down the block and Bruno followed me home."

She picked up Norman's crutch out of the yard and walked up the front steps. She put her suitcase on the front porch, helped him up, and handed him his crutch. She then dug keys out of her purse and opened the front door.

Kavitha picked up her suitcase and said, "C'mon."

Bruno trotted into the house after her and Norman followed, closing the door behind him.

Kavitha set down her suitcase in the foyer and said, "We're partners whether I live here or not. It's easier on you if I stay here. It's up to you. What's it going to be, Norman?"

"Stay," he said.

"Good choice," she said. She took off her coat and hung it in the coat closet, picked up her suitcase and trotted up the stairs. "Take a load off. I'll be back in a sec to make breakfast."

Norman went into the kitchen, opened the freezer, and grabbed a bag of frozen peas. He proceeded to the living room, leaned his crutch against the coffee table, and flopped down on the sofa. Gingerly, he positioned the bag of cold peas on his left knee.

Bruno peeped around a corner at him.

"Bastard," Norman muttered.

"What's with the frozen peas?" Kavitha asked.

"When your buddy bolted I fell and hurt my knee."

"That's too bad," she said. "Hobble your arse in here. Let's talk while I cook."

Still holding the bag of peas to his left knee, Norman picked up the crutch, positioned it in his right armpit, and complied.

Bruno was already in the kitchen when Norman entered, sitting pretty next to his food and water dishes. Kavitha took off Bruno's leash and hung it from the doorknob of the door to the garage. Shen then picked up the dishes, rinsed them in the sink, filled them, and set them back on the floor.

Bruno chowed down as Norman leaned his crutch against the kitchen table and sat down.

Kavitha opened the refrigerator and removed turkey bacon and Eggbeaters. She said, "What's all that paperwork on the table?"

"My TIAA – CREF account statement," he said.

"What's that?" she asked.

"Teachers Insurance and Annuity Association— College Retirement Equities Fund; my Folger retirement fund. You know Amherst College oversees the Folger's operations. That's why our paystubs are from Amherst College, and it's why Folger employees are eligible for TIAA – CREF."

"Right," she said. "How does it look?"

"Sweet," he said. "Even without the money I got from Rupert for the Shakespeare's BlackBerry heist, I'm looking pretty good. I can live comfortably in my retirement."

"That's great, Norm. Now, fill me in on the Voynich Manuscript."

She listened intently as she went about preparing breakfast.

Norman said, "The Voynich manuscript is an illustrated codex hand-written in an unknown writing system. The vellum on which it is written has been carbon-dated to the early 15th century (1404–1438), and it may have been composed in Northern Italy during the Italian Renaissance. The manuscript is named after Wilfrid Voynich, a Polish book dealer who purchased it in 1912. The first confirmed owner was Georg Baresch (1585–1662), an obscure alchemist from Prague, who postulated that the codex was a representation of Egyptian science.

"Some thirty pages of the manuscript are missing, with around 240 remaining. The text is written from left to right, and most of the pages have illustrations or diagrams. Some pages are foldable sheets. The overall impression given by the surviving leaves of the manuscript is that it was meant to serve as a pharmacopoeia or to address topics in medieval or early modern medicine.

"The Voynich manuscript has been studied by many professional and amateur cryptographers, including American and British codebreakers from both World War I and World War II. No one has yet succeeded in deciphering the text, and it has become a famous case in the history of cryptography. The mystery of the meaning and origin of the manuscript has excited the popular imagination, making the manuscript the subject of novels and speculation. None of the many hypotheses proposed over the last hundred years has yet been independently verified.

"In 1961, rare book dealer extraordinaire Hans Peter Kraus purchased the enigmatic manuscript for $24,500. After seven years of unsuccessfully attempting to sell it for as much as $160,000, he donated it to Yale University's Beinecke Rare Book and Manuscript Library in 1969, where it has been ever since, catalogued under call number MS 408."

Kavitha put breakfast on the table and sat down.

"Incredible, Norm."

"Why do you think Wolfgang Von Essen desires the manuscript?"

"Other than being a collector of antiquities and objets d'art? I don't know. We'll need to find out more about him."

Norman nodded

Kavitha said, "He *is* obsessed with good health. You said the manuscript may be some kind of pharmacopoeia. Maybe it contains cures for diseases that cannot be cured by modern science. Maybe he wants to be healthier…and also sell such cures to his filthy rich crowd."

Norman said, "That's a thought. Health *is* wealth."

"Uh huh. It's only fitting for the Master Race to have guaranteed good health."

Norman said, "Exactly. *If* he can decipher its mysteries."

"*If* we can steal it," she said.

"*If*, yeah. By the way: Are you working today?"

"Yes," she said.

"Apply for the position of part-time house manager. They always need help with performance venues and I'm going to need your help lifting the Voynich Manuscript from its display case in the Great Hall. We're going to heist it after intermission for the evening performance of whatever they are featuring during the Voynich exhibit."

"Why not just steal it in the middle of the night?" she asked.

"It's better if I do it while I'm working my shift, so my movements coincide with the execution of my duties. I'm going to change my shift from day work to evenings, like I did the night we went after the writing table. You will be executing your duties as a house manager when you help pull off the job, so you will also be above suspicion.

"Of course, we're going to have to see how things operate once the exhibit opens and we handle a few

92

intermissions. Once we have the timing down, we'll make our move."

Kavitha nodded and said. "You're the boss. I'll go in early and apply for a house manager position before I open the gift shop. "

Bruno sat and stared at Kavitha the whole time they ate breakfast.

After Kavitha put the plates, glasses, and flatware in the sink, she took the leash from the doorknob and said, "Okay, Bruno, let's go for a walk."

Bruno took his feet and pranced. Kavitha hooked his leash to his collar and they walked into the living room.

"Bastard," Norman mumbled.

[0000]

BLALOCK RESIDENCE
CAPITOL HILL

December 17th, 9:57 A.M.

Remus rang Romulus's Cell #1 and said, "Open the door, I'm right out front."

Norman disconnected the call and opened the front door.

A manila folder in hand, Luther sprinted up the front stairs.

"You look shook," Norman observed.

"Come on, let's go to the kitchen," Luther said.

Norman closed and locked the door and followed Luther into the kitchen.

Luther turned the faucets on full blast, held up the manila folder and said, "Wolfgang Von Essen – Essen with an "e" – is…a monster…or a demon…or something, far as I can tell."

"What are you talking about?"

Luther said, "Dude. Listen: Von Essen's birth certificate says he was born in Napa Valley, California on *March 16*, 1979. Filthy rich since then.

"He's a California vintner, owner and operator of Von Essen Vineyards, with a world-class Riesling. He is also an investment banker, with Wall Street, Deutsche Bank, and IMF connections. He's a trillionaire. But his birth certificate belongs to a boy who died at birth, according to the death record I cross-referenced his alleged birth certificate to.

"I had my buddy at NSA run Von Essen's photo through facial recognition..." Luther Kane trailed off. "It was positive for...Karl Richter. Dr. Karl Richter, born March 16, *1911* in *Essen*, Germany.

"Get this: he was assistant to Dr. Josef Mengele, *the* Dr. Josef Mengele, the Angel of Auschwitz. Richter was a pioneer in Aviation Medicine and Controlled Genetics. He was friends with Dr. Otto Ambros, Hitler's favorite chemist.

"Ambros helped create Sarin gas and synthetic rubber, for tires and tank treads, and solved the problem of the Reich's rubber shortage. Ambros had Jewish slaves manufacture the synthetic rubber at the Auschwitz/Birkenau Complex. The Fuhrer rewarded him with one million Reichsmarks. His friends ran Nordhausen, near Buchenwald concentration camp, where Jewish slaves built V-2 rockets.

"Originally he was a defendant in the Nuremburg Trials, but the U.S. Government had his name pulled from the list and he was recruited by the U.S. government to work as contractor for Operation Paperclip, along with 9,000 other Nazi scientists.

"To make it all palatable, the U.S. government told the American public that these Nazi butchers were 'the good Germans'.

"Richter was assigned to Randolph AFB in San Antonio, TX. He worked for MK Ultra, you know, the mind control experiments. Part of his claim to infamy is that he determined that children subjected to Psychic Trauma by age

3 and repeated by age of 6 would create a Dissociative State in such individuals and prime them for mind control, you know, like the Manchurian Candidate.

"Developed psychedelic mind control drugs and experimented on minorities at VA Hospitals and University of Pennsylvania. Performed microwave radiation and a variety of medical experiments on unsuspecting minorities. In fact, he was key in the Tuskegee Experiments.

"He also helped the U.S. Air Force develop pilot suits for high altitude aircraft, and helped NASA develop space suits.

"Recipient of the Department of Defense Distinguished Civilian Service Award, the highest award a scientist can receive. But he was behind the Tuskegee Syphilis Experiments."

Kane opened the folder and held it up for Blalock to see. He said, "The photo on the left is that of Dr. Karl Richter, taken circa 1943. The photo on the right is that of Wolfgang Von Hessen, taken last week."

Blalock was astonished that the photos appeared to be of the same man. He muttered, "But that would make him about 100 years old."

Kane said, "Yeah. But he looks to be in his early to mid-forties. Real Twilight Zone shit, am I right?" He closed the folder, put it back in his lap and said, "At one point, it appears he pretended to be his own son, going by the name Karl Richter, Jr.

"He *did* father Wolfgang Richter. Wolfgang wed Gretchen Müller and they produced Ida Richter…Von Essen's current wife. He's married to his own granddaughter!"

They were silent for a time.

Kane handed Blalock the folder and said, "I'll be in touch. Watch your six."

Luther turned off the faucets and walked toward the front door, Norman following.

[0000]

Norman declined Kavitha's offer to have people over for Thanksgiving. He did not wish to watch people enjoying themselves at a holiday feast while he dined on hospital food. The same for Christmas. She allowed him to have something other red wine on Christmas Eve, however. He enjoyed a couple of snifters of Hennessy. When he retired after midnight, she followed him into his bedroom and unwrapped his present. He suffered a bit of anxiety, because he thought he had no gifts to bring. Turned out he was wrong. They exchanged gifts and there was peace on Earth and good will between them.

On New Year's Eve, they had Luther and Nadia over. They played Poker, smoked cigars, and drank John J. Bowman Single Barrel Bourbon Whiskey. Kavitha even allowed Norman to eat a couple of greasy fried chicken wings smothered in Mumbo Sauce Luther had bought from a carryout on his way over.

Kavitha bit into one of the sauce covered wings and said, "Mmmm. This tastes good. It isn't good for you, but it tastes good. What is Mumbo Sauce?"

Norman said, "No one is sure. The ingredients are a Chinese secret. I can tell you this, though: I first had Mumbo Sauce at Wings and Things Carryout on Georgia Avenue, down the street from Howard University, so pretty much all of their regular customers were black. That joint was the birthplace of Mumbo Sauce.

"So, I'm standing at a counter sampling this delicacy, so I asked the proprietor, "Mama-San, what is Mumbo Sauce? It's delicious. She said in her thick accent, 'Can't tell you. Secret.' I thought, fair enough. Colonel Sanders has a secret recipe for Kentucky Fried Chicken. She didn't want to get ripped off. So I ask her why she named it that and she replied, 'Because you peepo mumbo.' I ran it around inside my head for a couple of seconds and then realized what she was saying, talking about black folks: Because you people mumble!"

They all had a good laugh on that one. They had lots of good laughs and brought in the new year right. A good time was had by all, in spite of the fact that he was dying for a cigarette the whole night. Drinking coffee or liquor always exasperated his cravings for cigarette smoke. Cigar smoking paled by comparison.

He was finally in the mood after midnight on the first day of the new year, and so he sat down at the piano, had Luther put on the turntable the 1958 album, *Ahmad Jamal at the Pershing; But Not for Me*, and accompanied the master pianist playing *Poinciana (Song of the Trees)*. Perfectly, Norman played the great Jazz Standard note for note. Kavitha and Nadia were impressed, but Luther was already familiar with his cousin's musical talent.

After their guests left, Kavitha pressed him to play one more song. Norman pulled out his *Donny Hathaway's Greatest Hits* album and handed it to her.

"Put this on and play the first cut," he said, and then sat down at his piano.

Kavitha complied and Norman not only played *A Song for You*, but sang along.

Kavitha exclaimed, "You can sing too!"

Norman smiled and continued to sing.

I've sung a lot of songs, I've made some bad rhymes
I've acted out my life in stages
With ten thousand people watching
But we're alone now and I'm singin' this song for you

When the song was over, Kavitha was crying. She took him by the hand to his bedroom. They closed the door in Bruno's face, and she showed him her appreciation.

On January 9th, Norman's cast was removed and he began rehab that same day. He was ordered to undergo rehab Mondays, Wednesdays, and Fridays, and he complied. It hurt like hell. That same day he got his cardiologist and his physical therapist to agree to release him to return to full duty in a couple of weeks, provided he did well in rehab and continued to its conclusion, and continued keeping his appointments with his doctors.

On January 12th, while Kavitha stayed warm in the Jag, parked near the entrance of B&W Stat Lab on the 3100 block of Georgia Avenue, N.W., Norman went inside at 6:00 A.M. to take his drug test for his special police officers license renewal. He was the first to be served and had gotten in line five minutes before the place opened. He got his results back in about twenty minutes and they were on their way.

That same day at around 9:00 A.M, Norman parked in Puck Circle and, forcing himself not to limp, went inside the Folger Library where he 1) met with Chief Leonard, obtained the ID he needed to log on to Pearson Vue's website so he could fill out and submit that agency's online forms and pay $84.00 with a personal credit card; 2) have Yvonne Barton notarize his Arrest Affidavit, swearing that he had not been arrested since his last license renewal, which he must submit to the Security Officers Management Branch along with the certified copy of his drug test results, and his Residence and Employment History form; and 3) saw Yvonne Davis in the Business Office and got reimbursed the $30.00 he'd paid B&W Stat Lab for the drug test. (The Folger would reimburse him the $84.00 he'd paid for his license with a check at a later date.)

On January 16th, Norman arrived at the Reeves Center at 3:00 A.M., where a line of special police officers and security officers seeking to renew their licenses had already formed, although the building would not open until 6:30 A.M., the Metropolitan Police Department Security Officers Management Branch (SOMB) could only process eighty-eight customers per day, so one must get there early to ensure getting one of those coveted slots. Norm was 25th in line.

Kavitha sat in the Jag parked on U Street at 14th Street, N.W., alongside of the building.

Frederick Douglass's walking stick in hand, bundled up like Matthew Henson, Norm brought along a lawn chair so that he would not have to stand in line for the long wait, and he and Kavitha took turns warming themselves inside the Jag, which was parked on U Street at 14th Street, N.W., alongside of the building, a half-hour at a time, until the building opened. He held the manila envelope containing the necessary paperwork for his license renewal as he sat in the lawn chair and she held the envelope when she sat in the lawn chair. Even bundled up in winter wear, she caused quite a stir among the other customers, of course. A little after 6:30 A.M, the customers were allowed access to the building, ordered to empty their pockets into a tray, pass through a metal detector, and finally were allowed to sign the SOMB visitors' log and be guaranteed their place in line when that office opened at 7:30 A.M. They then were promptly evicted from the building and told to return for service in one hour. Norman sat in the Jag until then. Upon reentering the Reeves Center, he and his colleagues once again had to go through the same screening process. In the SOMB, Norm waited his turn to be served, turned in paperwork and paid the cashier $35.00 for fingerprinting, got fingerprinted and photographed for his SPO license ID. Around 10:45, he was told he could leave and that his new license would be mailed to his employer to be issued to him before his current license expired.

[0000]

INTREPID DETECTIVE AGENCY
SOUTH CAPITOL AND N STREETS, S.W.
WASHINGTON, D.C.

January 16th, 6:31 P.M.

Norman Blalock parked his Jag on N Street alongside of the Intrepid Detective Agency, located atop The Last Stop Liquor Store on South Capitol Street, directly across from Nationals Park. His walking stick in hand, he and Kavitha climbed out of the car and closed the doors after them. Norman, looked up at the marquee as he adjusted his fedora and Kavitha pulled down her snug, short black skirt. They walked into the alley alongside the liquor store, Norman's cane tapping on the pavement, and up the side stairs to the office above the store.

On the way up, Kavitha asked, "Are you sure the bionic detective can help us?"

Norman answered, "If he can't no one can."

Kavitha stopped him mid-flight, spun him around, and looked him in the eye. In her lyrical British accent she pressed, "*Will* he? Even if he's willing, will he be *able* to help us?"

"Luther's good at this kind of work. Why wouldn't he?"

Kavitha seemed to be waiting for a better answer. Norman gave her one:

"Listen, he's family and he is capable. Not only is he trustworthy, but he was a cop and a soldier. And he's intrepid, like the sign says."

Kavitha shrugged and said, "Can't hurt to discuss it with him, I suppose."

Norman and Kavitha walked up the rest of the stairs and opened the office door. He let Kavitha enter first and closed the door after them.

The receptionist was a striking woman, a Raven-haired-swarthy-complexioned-shapely-young-beauty with arresting eyes the color of honey, crammed into a white silk blouse.

She spoke with a Russian accent. "How can I help you?"

"My name is Norman Blalock. I wish to speak with Luther Kane."

"Mr. Kane speaks to no one without an appointment."

"Just tell him I'm here, please."

The receptionist picked up the phone, pressed a button, and said, "There is a Mr. Blalock here to see you."

Momentarily, the door to Kane's private office swung open and Kane stepped out. He shook Blalock's hand while Netram looked on.

"Good to see you up and about, man," said Kane. "Good to see you, too, Kavitha."

"Likewise," said Kavitha

Luther said, "Come on in. Have a seat. Hold my calls, Nadia."

"What calls?" said Nadia.

Luther looked at Nadia sideways and then stepped back into his office.

Norman and Kavitha followed Luther into his office and the detective closed the door. Kavitha and Norm took the two chairs in front of the desk while Luther walked around to the other side and sat down. He grabbed a half empty bottle of John J. Bowman Single Barrel Bourbon Whiskey and offered, "Drink?"

Kavitha and Norman shook their heads.

Kane poured himself two fingers into a glass, tossed it back and then said, "Shoot."

"Ever heard of the Voynich Manuscript?" Norman asked.

Kane shook his head.

Norman continued, "The Voynich Manuscript is a 600-year-old book, acquired somewhere in Europe by rare book dealer Wilfrid Voynich in 1912. It's been radio carbon dated to the 1400s and no one has ever been able to decipher, 'the most mysterious book in the world.' It's priceless.

"It's coming to the Folger next month, on loan from Yale University. Someone is putting the squeeze on us to steal it."

Luther Kane sat back and said, "Fill me in, cuz and tell me how I can help you."

[0000]

GRAFFIATO RESTAURANT
707 6TH STREET, N.W.
WASHINGTON, D.C.

January 17th, 1:06 P.M..

Kavitha was enjoying her Burrata Salad when Afshar Ansary sat down at her table.

"Do you mind?" he asked.

"Yes, I do mind. I told you, I think I'm being followed. What do you want?"

"You know what I want."

"I told you, when I have information for you, I will contact you."

"Don't disappoint me, Dr. Netram. I will be in touch."

Ansary stood and walked out of the restaurant.

[0000]

FOLGER SHAKESPEARE LIBRARY
CAPITOL HILL
WASHINGTON, D.C.

January 18th, 0630 Hours.

Norman parked in Puck Circle, one of the Folger Library's two private parking lots. He exited and locked his car and then walked to the front on the building, concentrating on not limping.

He stood there for a while, looking the old girl over.

Clad in Georgia white marble quarried from Stone Mountain, the Folger is often misidentified by tourists and other passersby as one of the Library of Congress' buildings. Indeed, the Art Deco masterpiece is in perfect harmony with the architecture of the federal buildings that surround it. However, the treasure trove of rare and priceless English Renaissance books, manuscripts and objets d'art, which includes the largest collection of Shakespeare First Folios and Shakespeareana in the world, is not a public building, but a private research library for vetted scholars from around the globe.

On the west and east ends of the building are the library's two glass and cast aluminum double front doors that match the grilles over the tall windows above the bas-reliefs. The winged horse Pegasus is carved on the planters on either side of the staircase to these doors. Masks of Comedy and Tragedy are displayed above these doors, Tragedy on the east side, Comedy on the west.

Blalock walked up the stairs and entered the building, where he found Officer Lucien Thony posted at the front desk.

Officer Thony smiled and said, "Hey, looks who's back!"

Officer Thony stood and shook Lt. Blalock's hand. "Good to see you back."

"Thanks, Lucien. It's good to be back."

"How're you feeling?"

"Great," said Blalock. "I'm going to the locker room and then I'm going to clock in. We'll talk more when I come back."

"Solid," Thony said.

Norman walked up three steps into the Authorized Personnel Only section, opened the glass door on his left, and down the stairs. On Alpha Deck, he turned left, walked past the new **Louis Carew Memorial Command Center**; past the Photography Lab, down the long hallway known as "the tunnel," to the offices of Facilities Management, where the men's locker room is located. He unlocked his locker and stowed his gray overcoat and gray wool Newsboy/Cabbie cap. He donned his Folger police jacket, which bore the same Shakespeare family crest shoulder patches as his uniform shirt, and snapped on his **POLICE** baseball cap. He closed and locked his locker and then walked back to the Command Center. And then he noticed the office door could no longer be opened with a key. A key card system had been installed in his absence. He rapped on the door and momentarily, Officer John Morris opened the door.

"Hey, Lieutenant!" Morris said. "Good to see you."

"Thanks, Morris. It's good to see you, too."

"Lots of changes around here since you been gone."

"I see," Lt. Blalock said, looking around the command center, checking out the electronics closely. New CCTV monitors, new burglar and fire alarm systems, new computers. New office furniture, as well.

Blalock sat down at one of the computers and logged on. He was prompted to change his password and when he did, he logged on to *SalesForce*, T&A software, and clocked in.

He log out, turned to Officer Morris, and asked, "How do I get my key card? Who do I see?"

"Go to HR when they get in and they'll program a new photo ID for you. You're going to need one to get around here now since most of the doors now don't have regular locks. Until the HR personnel get to work today, you can use a spare key card." Morris opened a drawer and retrieved a key card numbered "1", attached to a lanyard. "Here you go, Lieutenant."

"Thanks, John."

Lt. Blalock took the key card and hung it around his neck. He then grabbed his radio, labeled "3", turned it on, and clipped it onto his belt.

"How is the current exhibit?" Blalock asked.

"*500 Years of Oxford Treasures* is great," said Officer Morris. "They have a thousand year old book on display. But the next exhibit is going to be a doozy. We have to beef up security for some book Yale is loaning us."

"Really?" said Blalock. "I'll have to get up to speed."

Just then, Blalock's cell phone rang. He saw that it was Luther calling and immediately answered it.

"What's up?"

"Step outside. Meet me on 3rd Street near the Capitol Police guard shack."

"Copy."

Blalock discontinued the call, told Officer Morris that he'd catch him later, and then exited the command center.

He turned left out of the tunnel, proceeded down the hallway past the Board Room, the offices of HR and IT, turned left past the kitchen, and exited into the back parking lot through Door 21.

Norman turned left and proceeded through the alley, past the United States Capitol Police guard shack, and then climbed into the passenger side of his cousin's black Chrysler 300.

Norman said, "You're here awfully early so you must have news for me."

Luther said, "I sure do."

Norman said, "Before we get to your news, you should know they're still using digital cameras supplied and maintained by Horus Security, Inc., are all over the building, their recorded images stored forever offsite, time and date stamped, always retrievable for review. But now they have upgraded from Horus Wadjit EX 9000 Series Cameras and Digital Video Recorders to the 10000 Series."

Luther said, "Damn. I could have accessed the 9000 Series remotely, but cannot access the 10000 Series offsite. You're going to have to hack it manually."

"How do I do that?" Norman wanted to know.

"Get the schematics for the system," Luther told him. "You'll find them in the building engineer's office. Find out where the CCTV system hub is located and take pictures of it. I will review the photos and give you what you need to override the system.

"How's your eyesight?"

"Twenty/fifteen. Why?"

Luther said, "Great." He pulled black framed eyeglasses from his shirt pocket and handed them to Norman. "These will be useful. The lenses are just plain glass." He took out his cell phone and told Luther to put on the glasses. He tapped on the cell phone screen and then showed it to Luther. "Check it out."

Norman saw whatever he looked at on the screen. He removed the eyeglasses and turned them on himself and saw his face on the cell phone screen.

"Say something."

Norm heard Luther's voice come from his cell phone. Norm said, "Four-score and seven years ago," and heard his voice coming from the cell phone.

Luther turned off the app and explained, "These are 1080P HD Covert Weatherproof DVR Video Recording

Glasses, with photo gray lenses and noise reducing microphone. As you can see, its signal can be broadcast, but it has an onboard 32GB TF card. Give me your Burner #1 and I'll sync them." Norman complied. While Luther synced the devices, he said, "You can broadcast and/or record the CCTV system hub so I can tell you how to override it. You can also record anything that can be used as evidence against the assholes coercing you into robbing the Folger. Now, the app has been downloaded to your burner. To activate the eyeglasses DVR, tap this." Norman watched as his cousin instructed him.

"Got it," said Norman

Luther returned Norman's cell phone. "Wear the glasses from now on. People will just assume that you need glasses now, old man."

Norman nodded and said, "Okay. Got anything else for me?"

Luther held up a manila folder and said, "Kavitha met with a guy at the Graffiato restaurant yesterday. Dick Johnson got some great photos of him. My buddy at NSA ran him through facial recognition software and identified him as one Afshar Ansary. He is employed by Omni Oil Consortium, listed as a consultant. But my friend at INTEROL tells me dude is a hitman.

"His passport records indicate that everywhere he travels, people causing the consortium problems have been assassinated. There is a detailed list in here. The last job he pulled was James Obano, leader of the Niger Delta. Obano was shot in Abuja Nigeria on November 9th.

"And here's the kicker: Ben Johnson was Ansary's mentor. Ansary was Johnson's got-to guy evidently."

Blalock said, "Let's finalize the arrangements we discussed in your office, set up the meetings. It's time for us to go to work."

Kane handed Blalock the folder and said, "Copy that. Watch your six."

Norman climbed out of the car and retraced his steps back to the Folger Library. He walked past Door 21 and went around to the Visitors' Entrance. There he ran into Nathan Rockford, standing at the bottom of the staircase to the Visitors' Entrance.

Rockford said, "Well, well. Look what the cat dragged in. And I thought I was the only one working here who likes to get in early."

"Captain," said Lt. Blalock.

"That's chief," said Rockford.

"Since when?"

"Since last Friday. Just kidding about calling me chief. Call me Rocky, just like always."

"What happened to Malcolm Leonard?"

"They let him go last Friday and promoted me on the spot. There's a new sheriff in town."

Norman nodded.

Chief Rockford said, "Maybe I should thank you for filing that EEOC complaint against him."

"Really?" said Blalock.

"He had other issues management wasn't pleased about. Your complaint may have been the straw that broke the camel's back."

"What's the official story?" Norm asked.

Rockford answered, "You know they don't need a story to let an at-will employee go. But for the official record, Chief Leonard retired."

Norman nodded.

"Morris was telling me we're beefing up security for the next exhibit. Bring me up to speed."

Chief Rockford said, "Yeah. Decoding the Renaissance. We're beefing up security because of some six hundred year old book called the...Fornich Manuscript. Something like that. Yale University is loaning it to us for the new exhibition, which opens February 4th. Damned thing has some kind of cult following. Yale University has been getting weird requests to view the thing for decades. I hear one nut requested to see the thing just for a few seconds, so he could lick some of its pages! Can you believe that? Yeah, we've got to take real good care of that thing."

Blalock said, "Bring me up to speed on the security upgrades."

"Sure," said Chief Rockford. "Let's walk and talk. Hey, I didn't know you wear glasses."

Norman shrugged.

The two walked up the steps, entered the building, and walked down the hall toward the chief's office.

"Any chance I can be assigned to the 3rd shift?" Blalock asked.

"Sure," said Rockford. "Sgt. Gary Thomas needs to work day work now."

The chief unlocked his office door and they entered. The place was in disarray, filled with packed boxes.

Blalock said, "Is it okay if I start tomorrow?"

Chief Rockford said, "Sure. You won't be in charge of the 3rd shift, though. Management created a new civilian position, Shift Supervisor, to operate the Command Center. They hired a new guy to fill the position about six weeks ago. Howard Stevens is his name. Great guy. Worked for the National Detective Agency for ten years; holds a master's degree in Criminal Justice and a bachelor's degree in computer science. Perfect to monitor all this high tech stuff we have installed in here."

"So, I have to answer to a civilian employee?" Lt. Blalock asked.

"That's right," said Rockford. "Essentially, he is the chief in the evenings."

Blalock said, "So, you're in charge on the 2nd shift. What about the 1st shift? Is there a shift supervisor for 1st shift?"

Rockford said, "No. Just the 3rd shift."

"Who operates the Command Center on 2nd shift?"

"Sgt. Baylor," said Rockford.

"Sergeant?"

"Yeah," said Rockford. "He got promoted last month, specifically to manage the command center on day work."

"So, Officer Morris operates the command center on 1st shift?"

"He and Officer Thony take turns," Chief Rockford explained.

Blalock said, "So, a sergeant operates the command center during the day while you're here, a trained civilian specialist, who essentially holds your rank, operates it on 3rd shift, and officers operate it overnight?"

"You've got it," said Chief Rockford.

Blalock sighed and said, "Okay." He motioned toward the boxes and said, "Looks like you're moving."

Chief Rockford said, "Yeah. My office is being relocated downstairs, to the office of the gift shop manager, and the gift shop manager is being relocated to the mail room, where they gave him a desk in the corner. This office here will accommodate two new central library employees."

Lt. Blalock said, "The gift shop manager's office is...kind of small, Chief."

Chief Rockford shrugged and said, "I don't need much space. Grab a box will you? Guys from Facilities are moving me out today, but we might as well take something down to my new office now since we're headed that way. Then we'll go to the command center and I'll familiarize you with the new CCTV and alarm systems."

Rocky and Norman each picked up a box. Norman followed the chief down the hall and down the stairs to Alpha Deck, to the chief's new, cramped quarters next to the mail room.

"Set it down anywhere," Rockford told Blalock.

Blalock put his box on the floor to the left of the door and Rockford put his box on the floor by his new desk.

The chief said, "Oh, Terrence Tiggle is now assigned to security."

Norman frowned and asked, "Why is the mailman assigned to security? Is he also a security officer now?"

The chief answered, "No. Just a realignment of personnel. His salary now comes out of our budget now. C'mon. I'll show you around the command center."

Norm followed Rocky into the command center next door, where they found Sgt. Frederick Baylor sitting at a computer in front of a bank of CCTV monitors.

"Look who's back," said Sgt. Baylor. "Need glasses now, huh?"

Blalock shrugged and shook Baylor's hand.

"Congratulations, sergeant," said Blalock.

"Thank you. How are you feeling?"

"Great," Norman lied.

"It's great to have you back."

"It's great to be back."

Chief Rockford said, "Let's bring him up to speed on the command center and our security upgrades, Sgt. Baylor."

"My pleasure," said Baylor.

Norman listened to Sgt. Baylor and Chief Rockford while they trained him on the operating systems of the new CCTV and alarms. Afterward, he read the operating manuals for the new systems, front to back.

Lt. Blalock went to the secure area outside the library's bank vault with Rosalind Larry at 0844 hours and they went through the gauntlet of high-tech security measures to gain access to the bank vault door sealing off the entrance to its underground treasure trove beyond a sliding bullet-resistant door via biometric verification of authorized personnel, implemented first by Ms. Larry and then by Lt. Blalock.

First, there is the palm print scanner, followed by facial and voice recognition protocols (last name first, first name last), and the Word-of-the-Day spoken by security personnel, which is always something to do with the Bard. (The password that morning was *Othello*). The final stage is the retina scanner in the wall next to a gate constructed of titanium bars situated in the entrance to the alcove containing the vault door. The gate opened just as the vault door's time lock disengaged at precisely 08:45. Ms. Larry twisted the dial back and forth until the four-digit combination code had been input, and then stepped aside to give Lt. Blalock room to spin the vault door's big wheel and then swing the massive metal door outward...

Norman perused the *500 Years of Oxford Treasures* exhibit when the Great Hall opened at 1000 Hours and then patrolled the building all day long, ignoring his throbbing ankle and making sure not to limp. All day long, his coworkers seemed pleased that he was back and told him so. Annie, Stephanie, Christina, Amanda, Francesca, Heather, and Marianne in the Box Office. Beth, Janet, Terri, Jennifer, Peter, and David in the Education Department. Docents Joe, Helen, and Diane. Alex Billups, Matt, and Luis from IT. Building Services Technician Arnie Caldeira. Melody Fetske, Director of Finance and Administration. Security Officer Wheeler. And so on.

Before he knew it, it was time to check off.

He went to the Command Center and found a bear of a man with the body of a wrestler talking with Sgt. Baylor.

Baylor said, "Lieutenant, this is Shift Supervisor Howard Stevens. Howard, this is Lt. Blalock."

Stevens shook hands and said, "Nice to meet you."

Blalock took back his crushed hand and said, "Likewise."

"I understand you're going to be working my shift," said Stevens.

"That's right," said Lt. Blalock

Stevens said, "I look forward to working with you."

"Yes," said Blalock. He sat down, logged on to a computer, accessed *SalesForce*, and clocked out. Before he exited the command center, he said, "See you tomorrow."

Stevens said, "See you later."

[0000]

BLALOCK RESIDENCE
CAPITOL HILL

January 18th, 5:37 P.M.

Bruno was all over Kavitha when she entered the house. She rubbed him and said, "Good boy. Good boy."

Norman came out of the living room, holding a book. He watched the two lovebirds, shaking his head.

"I got the house manager gig, Norm. I start next Tuesday."

"Excellent. I'm working evenings starting tomorrow and I've already got a handle on the new security upgrades. The new exhibit opens February 4th. That's when our work really begins."

"When did you start wearing glasses?"

"These have been in my locker at work for quite some time. Figured I should start wearing them."

"Okay. They're quite fashionable. Love those retro frames."

"Thanks."

"I'll get dinner started. C'mon, Bruno."

Bruno followed Kavitha into the kitchen.

Someone pounded on Norman's front door like the police and Bruno barked and came back to the foyer. Norman answered the door and found Rupert Whyte standing on his front porch.

"Where is it?" Rupert asked. "I told you I wanted the writing table the first day you went back to work."

Norman held back Bruno, stepped onto his porch, and closed the door behind him.

"I can't get to it during the day, Rupert. It's too busy. The area where I hid it is a beehive of activity during the day. And even if I could get at it, I wouldn't. I won't get it until I'm ready. I'll settle up with you and your employer on the same day."

"What?" said Rupert. "You still don't know who you're dealing with Norman. Shall I kill one of your children, just to show you I mean business?"

"Remember, Rupert, you're a businessman, not a murderer. Your boss Wolfgang Von Essen is a murderer though.

"What I will do is child's play compared to what Von Essen will do if you don't give him what he wants. He will kill your family one by one until you comply."

"I believe you. I still want you to tell him I want him to take delivery of the Voynich Manuscript personally."

"And why would he agree to do that? Meeting with you is unnecessary. I will deliver..."

"It is if he wants the Voynich Manuscript," Norman interrupted. "Tell him if he doesn't show I'll see to it that his wife learns that she is married to her own grandfather."

"What are you talking about?" said Rupert.

Norman continued, "Whether I'm dead or alive, I've made arrangements to ensure that his wife finds out the truth about him. Tell Von Essen that. He'll meet with me. And at the same time he gets what he wants, so will you. Understand? I intend to be rid of the both of you at the same time. I'll let you know when and where."

"You can't dictate..."

Norman cut Whyte off, "Don't threaten my children again or all bets are off. All you'll get is a bullet in the head. Your boss, too. And never come to my house again, Rupert. Never."

Norman went back into his house and slammed the door in Whyte's face.

Rupert said, "Cheeky bastard!"

"Was that Rupert?" Kavitha asked.

"Yeah," said Norman. "He wanted the writing table. I told him he'll get it when I'm ready to let him have it."

"That's not good, Norm. You don't know what he's capable of..."

"He can go to hell! And you, too."

Bruno started whining as Norman continued, "I'm sorry I met you two snakes! If he hurts one of my children, I'll blow his God damned head off! And you'd better watch your six, too." He turned his anger on the dog and told Bruno to shut up.

"Who do you think you're talking to, Norman? No one twisted your arm to take Rupert's deal. You could have turned him down. You're a criminal too, so you can stuff that holier than though attitude."

"I took the deal, yes, and I regret it. It was the second biggest mistake I made in my life. And I'd be dead by now if I hadn't died. Dying saved my life. It save me from dying at your hands, probably."

"Talk to me like that again and I *will* kill you. Wanker."

Norman marched back to the living room and left Kavitha standing in the kitchen doorway.

In the living room, Norman pulled Burner #1 from a pant pocket and speed-dialed Remus. When his cousin answered he said, "Set the meet for this Friday, 10:00 A.M., in the Great Hall of the Folger. Make sure all the principals are present."

Without waiting for a response from Luther, Norman discontinued the call.

[0000]

FOLGER SHAKESPEARE LIBRARY
CAPITOL HILL
WASHINGTON, D.C.

January 20th, 10:00 Hours

Lt. Norman Blalock met Luther Kane and four other well-dressed gentlemen in the west lobby.

"Welcome to the Folger," said Blalock.

Luther said, "Thank you. Allow me to introduce my friends. This is Bernard Adler, Richard Talley, Adam Vance, and Daniel Marlowe. Gentlemen, this is Lt. Norman Blalock, he's agreed to show us around."

Blalock and his new acquaintances shook hands and exchanged pleasantries.

Luther said, "I have never been here before. Have any of you?"

They hadn't.

"Then you're in for a treat," said Norman. "Let me show you the Great Hall. The current exhibit is *500 Years of Oxford Treasures*. It ends tomorrow so you just made it. This way, gentlemen."

Norman showed them highlights of the exhibition before he and his guests went into the Shakespeare Gallery, just off of the Great Hall. They stayed there, undisturbed, for approximately three minutes before they reentered the Great Hall.

Everything was going to Norman Blalock's plan thus far.

Three days before the Great Hall reopened, Norman contacted Rupert and told him to deliver the counterfeit Voynich Manuscript and to have Von Essen in the city standing by for delivery. Kavitha brought the spectacular fake home the following day. Norman took the counterfeit

Voynich to work inside of a black canvass messenger bag with shoulder strap and stowed it in his locker.

[0000]

As You Like It opened at the Folger Theatre on January 24th. The *500 Years of Oxford Treasures* exhibition ended on January 22nd and the Great Hall closed to the public for two weeks to facilitate the installation of the *Decoding the Renaissance* exhibit, featuring the Voynich Manuscript. Consequently, the house management staff was forced to sell concessions in the theatre lobby and in the Anne Hathaway Gallery on the floor below as they did not have access to the Great Hall where concessions are normally sold, making for cramped quarters for the hundreds of theatre patrons. Still, it gave Kavitha a chance to learn the ropes of the job of house manager.

Norman spent the two weeks getting ready for the heist. One night he gained access to the building engineer's office, found and photographed the electrical schematics for the building to ascertain the location of the IT closet containing the hub for the CCTV system, and then went to that IT closet, located on Beta Deck, and recorded the electrical panels via his 1080P HD Covert DVR Glasses so he could consult with Luther on how to override the system. And every night he got to know the various part-time house managers and observed how they worked. He also observed the work habits of Shift Supervisor Howard Stevens, and felt him out.

One of Stevens's habits might prove to be invaluable: His hobby was building ships in bottles, which he quite often did on his desk in the office during his shift. Perhaps he would be distracted from the cameras while concentrating on the intricate task at a moment opportune to the execution of the heist.

The exhibition, *Decoding the Renaissance: 500 Years of Codes and Ciphers* opened to the public on February 4th, but Lt. Blalock and his colleagues got to see it the evening before.

Norman marveled at the exhibits: *A Renaissance-Twentieth Century Connection*, showcasing top U.S cryptographers from the 1920s to the 1920s William and Elizabeth Friedman, who lived near the Folger Library, where they researched Renaissance ciphers; *Inventive Tools for Secret Communication*; *Alphabets and Substitution*; *Strengthening the Ciphers*; *Messages in A's and B's*; *Shakespearean Ciphers?*; *How Anything Can Signify Anything; Friedman and World War II Cipher Machines*; and last but not least, the most mysterious book in the world, The Voynich Manuscript, which the legendary code-breaker William Friedman himself could not decipher.

As Luther Kane had directed, the first night the Great Hall was opened to theatre patrons for the new exhibit, Kavitha pretended to drop her cell phone under the vitrine containing the Voynich Manuscript in order to take a photo of the new alarm transponder, so Luther would know what device would be necessary to override it and slave it to him rather than the alarm company.

When the Great Hall reopened to concessions, Norman continued to observe theatre operations and house management personnel. He liked watching Officer Peterson interacting with the cast of *As You Like It* as they made entrances to and exits from the theatre via the theatre lobby. It was a great cast, Norman thought. Lindsay Alexandra Carter as Rosalind; Kimberly Chatterjee as Audrey; Michael Glenn as Oliver; Will Hayes as Charles; Jeff Keogh as Adam and Corin; Aaron Krohn as Touchstone; Allen McCullough as Duke Senior and Duke Frederick; Brian Reisman as Silvius; Daven Ralston as Musician and Ensemble; Lorenzo Roberts as Orlando; Antoinette Robinson as Cella; Dani

Stoller as Phoebe; Tom Story as Jacques; and Cody Wilson as Dennis and William. He really enjoyed casing the joint.

By February 10th, Norman felt that they were ready to pull off the heist.

[0000]

FOLGER SHAKESPEARE LIBRARY
CAPITOL HILL
WASHINGTON, D.C.

February 11th, 22:55 Hours

Lt. Blalock was sitting at the front desk when the phone rang. He saw by the Caller ID it was an in-house call, from the Command Center. He answered it.

"Blalock."

"Officer Thony just called out sick," said Supervisor Stevens. "I can't stay, and this is one of the night's he works alone, because it's one of John Morris's days off. Can you cover the 1st shift tonight."

Blalock said, "Sure."

"Thanks, Lt. Blalock. I owe you one!"

"No problem," said Blalock. He hung up just as Kavitha came upstairs from Alpha Deck and stepped into the west lobby. "Lucien Thony called out sick. I have to cover his shift."

"Oh, wow," she said. "Is our meeting still on with your cousin tomorrow morning or are we going to postpone?"

"It's still on," he said.

She said, "Won't you be tired?"

"I'll be okay. Want to take the car and pick me up in the morning?" he asked.

"That's okay. I'll walk. See you when you get home."

Norman nodded and said, "See you in the morning.

[0000]

INTREPID DETECTIVE AGENCY
SOUTH CAPITOL AND N STREETS, S.W.
WASHINGTON, D.C.

February 12th, 11:11 A.M.

Luther pointed to a photo of a screen grab from Norman's DVR glasses, handed Norman a device and said, "Attach read lead here and the blue lead...there. Then press this button, let it record for at least thirty seconds, and then press this button. The video will then run on a continuous loop, and the Great Hall will appear to be empty. Got it?"

Norman said, "Got it."

Luther set aside that photo and turned to Kavitha, handing her another device. "Affix this under the Voynich Manuscript display case, as close as you can to the alarm transponder. Then it will be safe for you to swing open the case." He picked up another device known as double suction cups and demonstrated on a small pane of glass, "Place this in the middle of the left front side of the display case, engage the suction cups, like so, grab the handle, and swing the case open. After you've removed the original and replaced it with the copy, closed the door, remove the double suction cups, like so, and then retrieve the transponder override from beneath the case. Got it?"

"Got it," Kavitha said.

Norman said, "Kavitha, you've got to convince your coworkers to let you clear the Great Hall and put away the bar and cash register in the concessions closet so you'll have time to get inside the Voynich vitrine and make the switch. I'll be able to ride shotgun for you because I'll take care of the cameras before intermission starts."

"That shouldn't be a problem," said Kavitha. "The volunteer ushers will be back in the theatre to watch the second half of the play. Kate Abbott, *the* house manager is off tomorrow night, so just Sarah Leonard and I are the only house management staff working. She'll keep Q busy. They like to grab a smoke out front after intermission. They enjoy each other's company."

Norman said, "Sarah? The buxom brunette?"

"The very same," said Kavitha.

Norman said, "No shit. Yeah, that'll work. The Brunette Bombshell will keep Officer Peterson distracted."

"We make our move right after intermission."

Luther loaded their tools into a gray canvass messenger bag with a shoulder strap, and handed it to Norman.

"Good luck," Luther told them.

[0000]

CONGRESSIONAL CEMETERY
CAPITOL HILL
WASHINGTON, D.C.

February 13th, 9:11 A.M.

Norman parked on Potomac Avenue, S.E., and then he and Kavitha walked over to E Street, S.E. At 18th Street, they and entered Congressional Cemetery at the Gatehouse.

Norman said, "Welcome to historic Congressional Cemetery."

He filled her in as they proceeded down Congress Street:

"The cemetery encompasses 35 acres. Its articles of subscription were filed on April 7, 1807, making it the first national cemetery, fifty years before Arlington National Cemetery was created. These articles denied burial to

121

"infidels," and persons of color could not be interred within the area enclosed by the fence.

"The cemetery almost immediately became associated with the U.S. Congress. The first year, Connecticut Senator Uriah Tracy was interred here. In 1820, the vestry of the Christ Church set aside one hundred burial sites for members of Congress and their families, as well other government officials. Notable dignitaries, such as John Philip Sousa and J. Edgar Hoover, rest in peace here.

"By 1997, Congressional Cemetery was forgotten and neglected. Volunteers, including nearby residents, members of the armed forces, school groups, church groups, service associations, and descendant organizations, put in thousands of hours of work each year and rescued it.

"Now a National Historic Landmark, Congressional Cemetery is once again an active cemetery and is flourishing. The brick pathways and slate walks have been restored to their original beauty.

"I'll tell Whyte and company that I'll meet them near the Mary McLeod Bethune statue in Lincoln Park, but at the last minute, I'll tell them we're meeting here, near the chapel. Near this gravesite."

Kavitha smiled when she read the name of the large grave marker: **WHYTE**. "Nice touch," she said.

"I thought so," he said.

On the way out of the cemetery, Kavitha pointed to a tall building located on Massachusetts Avenue and asked, "What's that?"

As they walked back to his Jag, Norman told her, "That used to be D.C. General Hospital, the city's first and only public hospital. Originally, it was the Washington Infirmary, circa 1806. In 1846 it came to be known as the Washington Asylum, and served indigent patients. In 1922 it became the site of the Gallinger Municipal Hospital. In 1953, it was renamed District of Columbia General Hospital.

"D.C. General closed a couple of decades ago. Now it's known as the D.C. General Health Campus, consisting of a number of clinics, including the Southeast Sexually Transmitted Diseases Clinic, the Detoxification Center, and the Women's Services Clinic."

"Interesting," Kavitha said.

Norman said, "Do you know a man by the name of Afshar Ansary?"

"No," Kavitha lied. "Why?"

Norman said, "Apparently, Ben Johnson was his mentor. He was Johnson's go-to guy when the Omni Oil Consortium needed troublemakers taken out of the equation. Supposed to be a hell of a sniper. Anyway, Luther tells me he's in town."

"Does Luther know why this...Ansary is here?"

"We suspect that he's looking into the death of his mentor. I'd hate to be in Rupert's shoes if Ansary suspects he had something to do with his mentor's death. I'd hate to be Rupert's employer, too."

"Me too," said Kavitha.

[0000]

FOLGER SHAKESPEARE LIBRARY
CAPITOL HILL
WASHINGTON, D.C.

February 13th

Norman called Rupert Whyte at 19:57 Hours and said, "Tonight's the night. You and Von Essen meet me at midnight in Lincoln Park, near the statue of Mary McLeod Bethune."

He did not wait for a response, he just hung up.

At 20:00 Hours, Lt. Blalock entered the Command Center.

Shift Supervisor Howard Stevens was doing delicate work with his bear paws, building a pirate ship in a bottle.

"Need a break, Howard?"

"Yeah," said Shift Supervisor Howard. He set down his tools and removed the magnifying eyeglasses he wore for this detailed work. He closed his eyes, rubbed the bridge of his nose, and then stood and stretched.

"Take fifteen minutes," Lt. Blalock told him.

"Thanks," said Howard.

Norman said, "Remember, I came in at 13:00 hours today, so I'll be clocking out at 21:00 hours. I'll stick around until after intermission, though."

"Got it," said Howard. "Thanks."

As soon as Howard left the room, Blalock sat down at the controls of the CCTV camera system. He selected the camera on Beta Deck in the hallway that covered the IT closet containing the CCTV hub, and then manually adjusted the camera in order to create a blind spot he could exploit so he could reach the IT closet without being caught on camera.

When Howard returned around 20:15 Hours, Blalock told him he was going to make his rounds.

Blalock exited the Command Center, turned left out of the tunnel, and left, up the stairs to the first floor. He turned left again and entered the Registrar's Office, proceeded through the Gail Paster Reading Room, through the half-door next to the Librarian's Desk, and through a wooden door leading to a stairwell. He ran down two flights of stairs to Beta Deck. Key card in hand, he unlocked a metal door, and slowly opened it. He'd looked around the space on the other side of the door to make sure that he was alone and then entered, closing the door after him. He then ran over to a wooden door directly ahead of him, unlocked it, and went through. He ran down the hallway to another wooden door, unlocked it, went through, and then turned right and proceeded down the stacks. Halfway down this passageway, he turned sideways and stayed close to the stack on the left to take advantage of the camera's blind spot he'd created, all the way to the IT closet. Carefully, he took the old fashioned key to that door he'd pocketed earlier during his shift, and let himself in, closing the door behind him.

He turned on the light and pulled from his jacket pocket the device Luther Kane had provided him. He attached the leads as instructed, accessed the Great Hall camera feed he needed, and made a thirty second recording. He then played back the footage on a loop.

Blalock turned off the light, slipped out of the IT closet, and then exited Beta Deck through Door 1. He turned left and ran up the steps, turned left again and ran to the men's locker room. He opened his locker, retrieved the black canvass messenger bag and the gray canvass messenger bag, locked his locker, and then ran out of the locker room, back down the stairs past Door 1, up the stairs to Door 12, proceeded up the stairs to Door 34, which could only be opened from the other side. He stowed the messenger bags in a trash can and then retraced his steps.

Intermission began at 20:45 Hours. Lt. Blalock entered the west lobby, said hello to Officer Sumorry Alpha, who was manning the front desk, and hello to the gift shop cashier, Erin Williams. He then walked through the Great Hall toward the east lobby, through the crowd of theatre patrons flooding into the exhibition hall to purchase concessions and peruse the *Decoding the Renaissance: 500 Years of Codes and Ciphers* exhibit. Part-time house managers Sarah Leonard and Kavitha Netram, assisted by volunteer ushers, waited on the customers while Officer Peterson manned his post in the theatre lobby. Norman made sure to catch Kavitha's eye and give her a nod, signaling her that they were all set.

Norman ran into Corinne Vigletta, Assistant Director of the Education Department, who happened to be attending the play. To his surprise she hugged him.

She said, "Good to see you back in action, Norm!"

He thanked her and assured her that he was okay when she inquired. He chatted with her for a while and then pressed on.

He caught Officer Peterson's eye and returned his thumbs up. Peterson walked into the Great Hall. They talked briefly and then Peterson asked, "How much longer do you plan to work here?"

Blalock shrugged and said, "Not much longer."

Peterson nodded and said, "Good. I worked three decades for the police department and then six years here. I'll be leaving in June. It's time to hang it up, my friend. Get business living. Get busy retiring."

Blalock agreed.

As usual, intermission was over quickly. The house lights flashed indicating it was time for the patrons to return to the theatre and they began to file out of the exhibition hall. Officer Peterson returned to his post.

Norman watched Kavitha talking with her coworkers and then the volunteer ushers and the Brunette Bombshell left the Great Hall. The volunteers went back into the theatre and the Brunette Bombshell and Q went out front for their smoke break.

Norman motioned to Kavitha and she rolled the bar over toward the Shakespeare Gallery, where the concessions closet sat off from it. He ran through the Shakespeare Gallery, down the hall past the concessions closet to Door 34, unlocked it, and retrieved the messenger bags. He ran back to Kavitha, opened the gray canvass bag, and handed her the tools.

"Go," he said. He took the bar from her control and wheeled it into the concessions closet while she lied on the floor in front of Vitrine 15, the Voynich case. She affixed the transponder override under the case, close to the alarm transponder, and stood up.

Norman joined her, keeping an eye out for any interlopers. He took the double suction cups from the gray messenger bag and handed it to her. She affixed the suction cups as instructed and carefully, pulled open the case. She reached inside and removed the Voynich Manuscript.

Norman pulled the duplicate Voynich from the black messenger bag and handed it to her. She in return handed him her copy, which he put inside the black messenger bag. She then put her copy inside the vitrine.

He said, "Open it to the right page. It's got a bookmark. That's it. Hand me the bookmark and close the case."

She complied and then removed the double suction cups and handed it to him.

"Get the transponder override," he said.

She complied and handed it to him and he put it in the gray messenger bag.

Norman said, "Finish putting away the stuff. I'll meet with Rupert and Von Essen. You stay here…"

"What?"

"Stay in the offices of the gift shop until after midnight. You'll be safe there."

Norman ran back down the hallway and disappeared through Door 34. He retraced his steps back to Door 1, unlocked it, entered, and then unlocked and entered the IT closet. He switched on the light, stopped the video replay, and disconnected the device. He stuffed it into his jacket pocket, switched off the light, and left the closet.

He went through Door 1 and ran upstairs to the men's locker room where he swapped out his uniform jacket and cap for his gray overcoat and gray Newsboy/Cabbie cap, and closed and locked his locker. He withdrew his Snub-nosed Bulldog .357 Magnum   five-shot, confirmed that it was loaded, and then stuffed it back into his coat pocket. Once again he retraced his steps, the two canvass messenger bags in tow.

Outside Double Door 34 leading to the rear parking lot, Luther Kane was waiting for him. They ran from the Folger rear parking lot to Luther's black Chrysler 300, which was parked on A Street, S.E. Luther unlocked the car with his remote, they climbed in, and drove away.

[0000]

CONGRESSIONAL CEMETERY
CAPITOL HILL
WASHINGTON, D.C.

February 13th, 23:40 Hours

When Norman entered the cemetery at 11:15 P.M., he'd called Whyte and told him the time for the meet was the same, but the location had been changed. He told Whyte to enter Congressional Cemetery on E Street, S.E., at 18th, at the Gatehouse, and proceed down Congress Street to the chapel, where they would find him.

As soon as he'd disconnected the call, snow began to fall.

Whyte and Von Essen came early, just as he knew they would. The moment they stepped into view out of the night, lightning flashed and thunder rumbled. A thundersnowstorm was upon them.

As Whyte and Von Essen approached him, Norman said, "Welcome to historic Congressional Cemetery, gentlemen."

"Where is Kavitha?" Rupert asked, looking around.

Norman said, "She couldn't make it. She's got something better to do. Guess you missed the memo. Besides, we don't need her here to conduct our business."

"True," said Rupert. He smiled when he read the name on the large grave marker Norman was standing next to: **WHYTE**. He pointed at the marker and told Norman, "Nice touch."

Norman said, "I thought so."

Von Essen said, "Where is it?"

"You arrived early. It isn't here yet. It's on its way, though. My colleague will ring me when he arrives and stay on the phone with me to make sure nothing untoward happens to me before he gets a chance to deliver it. Kill me and you get nothing."

"He has my purchase also, I suppose," said Whyte.

"Of course, Rupert. Like I told you, I will conclude my business with both of you tonight."

"How long must we wait?" Whyte sighed.

"I told you to meet me at midnight," said Norman. He glanced at his wristwatch and said, "You're twenty minutes early."

Von Essen said, "Despite the fact that you decided to show up alone, it would appear that you are a very cautious fellow, Mr. Blalock."

Blalock said, "Have to be when dealing with people like you."

"That is wise," Von Essen agreed. "Although I must admit that this is a very interesting choice for a meeting place."

Blalock said, "I'd considered having our meeting at the Albert Pike statue in Judiciary Square. Do you know him?"

Von Essen smiled and said, "Yes, of course."

Whyte shook his head and asked, "Who is he?"

Norman said, "General Albert Pike is the only Confederate military officer with an outdoor statue in Washington, D.C., standing in front of police headquarters, a stone's throw away from D.C. Superior Court.

"Aside from being a soldier who served faithfully during the Mexican-American and Civil Wars, he was, among other things, an attorney, a journalist, a poet, a mass murderer, and, allegedly, a Grand Wizard of the Ku Klux Klan. Some even believe he actually founded the KKK.

"In 1862 Pike allegedly commanded Sioux Indian warriors to murder some 800 Protestants in the town of New Ulm, Minnesota, while the men were off serving in the Union Army. Officially in charge of this military tactic, he organized and implemented several such attacks while serving in the Confederate Army, evidently in collusion with the Jesuit Pierre De Smet, whose influence over Native Americans was legendary.

"An eminent and influential 33rd Degree Freemason, Pike served as Sovereign Grand Commander of the Scottish Rite's Southern Jurisdiction for thirty-two years.

"In 1871, he published *Morals and Dogma of the Ancient and Accepted Scottish Rite of Freemasonry* to educate Freemasons to the deeper meanings of Freemasonry. He also wrote, *The Aryan Race: Country, Character and Manners of the Indo-Aryans.*"

Von Essen nodded knowingly.

Norman continued, "*In Morals and Dogma*, Pike wrote, 'We shall unleash the nihilists and the atheists and we shall provoke a great social cataclysm, which in all its horror will show clearly to all nations the effect of absolute atheism; the origins of savagery and of most bloody turmoil.

"'Then everywhere, the people will be forced to defend themselves against the world minority of the world revolutionaries and will exterminate those destroyers of civilization and the multitudes disillusioned with Christianity whose spirits will be from that moment without direction and leadership and anxious for an ideal, but without knowledge where to send its adoration, will receive the true light through the universal manifestation of the pure doctrine of Lucifer brought finally out into public view. A manifestation which will result from a general reactionary movement which will follow the destruction of Christianity and Atheism; both conquered and exterminated at the same time.'"

Von Essen said, "Yes. I must say that it is astonishing to me that a schwartza knows Albert Pike, and is so well versed in his doctrine. Perhaps you even understand the way the world truly works. Extraordinary.

"Herr Pike also said, 'Fictions are necessary for the people, and the Truth becomes deadly to those who are not strong enough to contemplate it in all its brilliance. In fact, what can there be in common between the vile multitude and sublime wisdom? The Truth must be kept secret, and the masses need a teaching proportioned to their imperfect reason.' I agree."

Norman said, "Spoken like a true Knight of the Golden Circle.

"Yes, standing beneath the statue of Albert Pike would have been a more suitable place for our meeting. Do you not agree, Herr Richter? That is your real name, isn't it? You *are* Dr. Karl Richter of the Third Reich, correct?"

"Yes," Von Essen said proudly.

"What?" said Whyte. "Dr. Karl Richter is dead."

"No, Rupert. He's standing right there. Dr. Mengele's right-hand man. Your friend here has found the fountain of youth, apparently.

"How are you cheating death, Herr Richter?"

"I have always been interested in increasing human lifespan. My colleagues and I sought the secret of longevity, with the ultimate goal of obtaining immortality.

"We made scientific breakthroughs through human experimentation..."

"On Jews in concentration camps," said Norman.

Von Essen smiled and said, "Certainly. Jews and other mud people. Our work continued in America after the war..."

"The Tuskegee Syphilis Experiment," Norman interrupted.

"Yes. And other experiments. However we did not confine our research to modern science. We sought ancient secrets, as well. Alchemy. Herbalism. The Occult.

"But long before the rise of the Third Reich, I made significant progress. In 1930, I traveled to Kai Xian, Sichuan, Republic of China to follow up on a 1930 New York Times article about Li Ching-Yuen. According to the article, Wu Chung-Chieh, a Chengdu University professor, discovered Imperial Chinese government records from 1827 congratulating Ching-Yuen on his 150th birthday, and further documents later congratulating him on his 200th birthday in 1877.

"I found Ching-Yuen, who stood some 2.1 metres in height. That's about seven feet tall. He told me of his remarkable life.

"Ching-Yuen died from natural causes in May of 1933. He was 256 years old, more than twice the age of France's Jeanne Louise Calment, who lived a mere 122 years."

Rupert laughed.

"I'm not joking," Von Essen snapped. "Look him up."

"I don't need to," said Blalock. "By the age of ten Li Ching-Yuen had traveled extensively in Tibet, Manchuria, Shansi, Annam, Siam, and Vietnam, gathering herbs. He claimed that his diet of herbs such as goji berry, lingahi, wild ginseng, gotu kola, and he shoo wu, and rice wine were the secret to his longevity.

"He was survived by his 24th wife and about two hundred descendants."

Von Essen was impressed. "Yes! His research yielded remarkable achievements. I added his research to my own and adopted his diet, with a few refinements.

"However, what I learned from Li Ching-Yuen was nothing compared to what I learned from the complete

Voynich Manuscript. I've learned the cures to deadly diseases, including the deadliest disease of all: aging.

"The book I gave you to substitute for the genuine article, which is also incomplete, is an exact copy of it, painstakingly made by an obscure Franciscan monk, assigned the task by the Collegio Romano, under the patronage of Pope Gregory XIII.

"The monk copied every page available to him, *after* twenty-eight pages of the codex had been removed from the original manuscript by an ambitious papist in order to conceal its precious secrets. Like the original, the copy was written with quill pen and iron gall ink on parchment made from calf skin and bound and covered in goat skin, and the blue, green, white, and red-brown paints used for the illustrations all match the original's perfectly.

"I acquired this perfect copy, along with the missing pages from the original manuscript, quite fortuitously, from the mansion of a billionaire Jewish scholar and avid collector of rare manuscripts. He was living in Berlin when the Third Reich seized his property and all of his assets in 1938 . I discovered these treasures when I claimed his home as my own and took inventory. In a few years, I deciphered the book."

Blalock said, "I don't understand. If you've already deciphered its secrets, why do you need the original Voynich Manuscript?"

Von Essen snapped, "I don't need it, I *want* it! And what I want, I take. I deserve that book. It belongs in my collection, where it can truly be appreciated. Like all of the other rare and priceless artifacts I have assembled over the course of a century, the secrets of the Voynich Manuscript are not meant for the eyes of puny men."

Norman said, "You've shared its secrets with your Nazi buddies, I'll bet."

Von Essen said, "To a chosen few, yes."

"For a price," said Norman.

"Certainly," said Von Essen. "Life is not cheap."

"Unless you're not white," said Norman.

Von Essen chuckled. "That is true. The world is overpopulated, too many mud people wasting precious resources and breathing room! A culling is necessary. The weak must make way for the strong!"

Norman said, "It wouldn't surprise me if you told me you were one of the chief designers of the Denver International Airport, where the chosen will ride out Armageddon. And of course, you're a zealot of the Project for the New American Century no doubt."

Von Essen smiled and said, "Better. The New World Order, the Fourth Reich."

"With you as the führer?" Norman asked.

"Well and why not? No man is more qualified than I."

Norman smiled and said, "You mean no superman. No mere mortal can compare to you, Herr Richter."

Von Essen laughed and said, "You are of course referring to Friedrich Nietzsche's superman philosophy, not the comic book character, yes?"

"Natürlich," said Blalock. "There certainly isn't anything funny about you, Herr Richter."

Rupert interrupted, "I say, old man, I could use a bit of that fountain of youth."

Von Essen said, "We will discuss that later."

Rupert smiled and said, "Good show!"

Norman said, "You may be able to extend your life, maybe even indefinitely, Herr Richter, but you're not immortal. Death *always* wins. Always."

"We shall see," said Von Essen.

Norman nodded and said, "We shall.

"I recall Einstein left Germany when Hitler rose to power, declaring that 'science and justice were now in the hands of a raw and rabid mob of Nazi militia.' Tell me, Herr Richter, does accomplishment cancel past crimes?"

Von Essen smiled and said, "Jedem das Seine?"

Norman translated, "Does everyone get what he deserves? That is the question."

Von Essen's eyebrows rose and he said, "Sie sprechen Deutsch!"

Norman replied, "Ich spreche viele Sprachen, Herr Richter."

Von Essen said, "Du bist was besonderes schwarza!"

Norman said, "Danke."

Blalock's phone rang and he answered, "Yes. Come ahead. I'll leave the line open."

Von Essen rubbed his hands together and grinned.

Luther Kane, gun hand dug deep inside his coat pocket, two canvass messenger bags strung by their shoulder straps over his left shoulder, strolled up from behind Norman Blalock, approaching from the opposite direction the Nazis had come through the cemetery, and stood beside his cousin, opposite Rupert Whyte and Wolfgang Von Essen.

"Hand them over," Blalock told Kane.

Kane walked over to them and handed the gray bag to Von Essen and the black bag to Whyte. He then backed away from them, back to his place beside his cousin. His gun hand never left his coat pocket.

Von Essen and Whyte hurriedly opened the bags and removed the contents. The smiles faded from their faces as they examined their prizes.

"This is the copy I gave you," Von Essen hissed.

Whyte yelled, "This isn't the writing table I wanted!"

"Kill them!" Von Essen yelled to his henchmen in hiding.

"Take them, gentlemen," said Norman into the wire he was wearing for the FBI.

FBI Emergency Response Team members dressed in black and armed with assault weapons came out of nowhere and surrounded Von Essen and Whyte.

Joe Whitehead, the ERT commander, yelled at Whyte and Von Essen, "Don't move! Show us your hands! Show us your hands! On your knees! On your knees!"

Shocked, Von Essen and Whyte complied. ERT members cuffed their hands behind them as Joe Whitehead told them they were under arrest for a laundry list of felonies, and then read them their rights.

A group of well-dressed gentlemen escorted by ERT members exited the chapel and strode over to the suspects. Luther Kane's operatives, Private Investigator Dick Johnson and Private Investigator Baby Jane Watson approached from another direction, escorting two handcuffed prisoners, Von Essen's henchmen. Dick Johnson was half his prisoners' height...and Baby Jane Watson's height, too.

"Got some more partygoers here for you," P.I. Johnson announced.

"They were waiting to ambush these officers of the court," P.I. Watson added.

"Get over there," P.I. Johnson told his prisoners. Johnson handed the gunsels guns to one of the ERT members.

Rupert said, "What's all this then?"

"This is absurd," Von Essen protested. "Release me!"

One of the well-dressed men who had stormed out of the chapel introduced himself to Whyte and Von Essen, "I am Bernard Adler, Assistant U.S. Attorney for the District of Columbia. We have arrest warrants charging you with multiple local and federal charges, from Cultural Property Theft to Conspiracy to Commit Murder..."

"Murder!" said Whyte. "Who said anything about murder?"

Blalock tapped the screen of his cell phone and showed Whyte video of him taken in front of the Blalock residence on the evening of January 18th, time and date stamped:

"You still don't know who you're dealing with Norman. Shall I kill one of your children, just to show you I mean business?"

"Remember, Rupert, you're a businessman, not a murderer. Your boss Wolfgang Von Essen is a murderer though.

"What I will do is child's play compared to what Von Essen will do if you don't give him what he wants. He will kill your family one by one until you comply."

"I believe you."

Norman stopped the video and put away his cell phone.

"Idiot!" Von Essen told Whyte.

AUSA Adler said, "You've been read your rights. You *do* have the right to remain silent. I suggest you exercise that right."

Blalock told Adler, "Please honor the special circumstances for chain of custody we agreed upon for these priceless artifacts."

"Of course," said AUSA Adler. "You remember Richard Talley of Lloyd's of London, the insurer for the Folger Library."

Blalock nodded and Talley returned the nod.

Adler continued, "He will take possession of the treasures and will retain control of said treasures while we videotape the evidence, and he will return the items to the library this morning. He, along with representatives from my office and the Department of Justice, will explain to your employer that even though the lives of your loved ones were threatened, you alerted the authorities of the conspiracy to commit the heist, and received special deputation from the U.S. Marshals Service to act as an officer of the court and actively safeguard said treasures."

Norman said, "You should look into that copy of the Voynich Manuscript he wanted me to swap for the original. If he obtained it legally, it's his personal property. If not, then that's another offense you can add to the laundry list of charges."

Another well-dressed man shook Blalock's hand and said, "You remember me, Adam Vance, Assistant Director of the Washington Field Office of the FBI. I will be sitting in on that briefing with your employer. I will tell them they owe you a debt of gratitude."

Daniel Marlowe, Deputy Director of the U.S. Marshals Service, shook Blalock's hand and chimed in, "I'll be in that meeting today with your employer, as well. Hell, as far as I'm concerned, you spearheaded this task force, and I'm going to let it be known."

"Oh, Bollocks!" Rupert exclaimed.

Norman said, "Thank you both."

"My pleasure," said Adam Vance and Daniel Marlowe.

Talley told Blalock, "You are also entitled to a finder's fee, so to speak, equal to ten percent of the value of the recovered items. The writing table is valuable and will fetch a pretty penny, but this…" – Talley reached inside the gray canvass messenger bag authorities had just seized from Von Essen and removed a small hardcover book – "…this last known quarto of *Titus Andronicus* is priceless."

Norman told Luther, "It's all yours, man. It was you who made this plan work."

Luther said, "Damn! What's ten percent of priceless, Norm?"

Norman said, "A shitload. And it's all yours."

Luther grinned from ear to ear.

Rupert protested, "I…we didn't force you to steal that quarto or that writing table!"

Adler said, "Oh? What *did* you try to force him to steal?"

Rupert turned red in the face and said, "What I meant to say was…"

"Just shut up!" Von Essen snapped.

Adler told the ERT commander, "Take them away."

The criminals and their entourage walked toward the cemetery's Gatehouse exit.

[0000]

Valentine's Day

12:05 A.M

Afshar Ansary had arrived at the D.C. General Health Campus an hour early and had tampered with the buildings camera surveillance system, setting the camera feeds for the roof and all along his entrance and escape route on the ground floor on prerecorded loops so he would not be seen. Now he was perched atop the main building, his impressive weapon resting on its bipod on the edge of the roof. Ansary adjusted the ATN X-Sight Day/Night Riflescope of his 7.62 QDC sound suppressor equipt Knights Armament SR-25 .308 Winchester sniper rifle. He sharpened the image of his primary target, Rupert Whyte, who was walking next to his secondary target, Wolfgang Von Essen, in the custody of law enforcement officer, roughly 321 metres down range. Today Afshar was using Lapua Subsonic Ammo, 200 grain.

[0000]

On the 1800 block of E Street, SE, as they were walking the prisoners to the transport vehicle, Wolfgang Von Essen flexed and snapped the chain link holding together his stainless steel handcuffs and freed his hands, which had been restrained behind his back. Pandemonium ensued as he grabbed and tossed big, beefy federal agents around like ragdolls. Richter's henchmen took advantage of the situation and ran off, their hands still cuffed behind them.

Under the raging thundersnow, Karl Richter Wolfgang Von Essen continued to manhandle law enforcement's finest, snapping arms, busting lips. and breaking heads. When the crowd thinned, he turned his attention toward Norman. Luther Kane drew his Colt .45 Model 1911 and Norman Blalock drew his Snub-nosed Bulldog .357 Magnum as Richter came toward them. But someone reached out and touched the beast from a distance and saved them the trouble. Richter's head exploded and his corpse dropped to the ground like a sack of cement right in front of them. An instant later, Rupert Whyte shared the same fate. No one heard the gunshots.

Luther's operatives Dick Johnson and Baby Jane Watson, who had started yelling, "What the hell!" and "Sweet Jesus!" the moment Von Essen broke free and went berserk, immediately took cover along with everyone else. Battered law enforcement personnel aimed their weapons in all directions, not having the faintest idea the direction from which the gunfire had come.

Luther Kane's operatives continued to yell, "What the hell!" and "Sweet Jesus!" well after the action was over.

Lying on the pavement, using the FBI ERT van for cover, Norman stared at the corpses of Rupert Whyte and Wolfgang Von Essen and whispered, "Checkmate, assholes."

Lying on the ground next to his cousin, Norman looked directly into Von Essen's dead eyes and said, "Jedem das Seine."

"What?" Luther asked.

Norman turned to his cousin and told him, "It means, 'Does everyone get what he deserves?'"

Luther nodded and said, "They got away with foul shit for a long time. But you can't outrun yourself. Everywhere you go, there you are." He looked around and then said, "Hey, I think the shooting is over."

Private Eye Luther Kane picked up his fedora off the ground and stood up. He dusted off his hat and put it back on as Norman rose to his feet.

Kane's operatives continued screaming, "What the hell!" and "Sweet Jesus!" long after the action was over.

When Private Eye Baby Jane Watson and Private Eye Dick Johnson finally stopped yelling and got up off the ground, Dick said, "Is he dead? Are y'all sure he's dead? Make sure he's dead."

Bloody and groaning, those battered law enforcement officers still capable of standing slowly staggered to their feet. Norman knew for a fact that not one of them would believe, nor even admit it if they knew it was true, that they'd had their asses handed to them by a hundred-year-old man.

[0000]

Afshar abandoned the sniper rifle on the roof. He immediately proceeded to a rooftop door a short distance away, sprinted down the stairs to ground level, and exited the building through a back door.

On the 1800 block of C Street, S.E., Afshar Ansary unlocked his black Chevy Impala rental car, climbed behind the wheel, and started the engine. He turned on the headlights. The last thing he saw before the bullet smashed through the windshield and struck him in the forehead was her, aiming a silencer equipt pistol at him.

[0000]

BLALOCK RESIDENCE
CAPITOL HILL

February 14th, 9:57 A.M.

As Bruno looked on, Kavitha was all over Norman as soon as he entered the kitchen via the door to the garage.

"What happened? I've been calling and texting you all night!"

Norman walked over to the kitchen table, pulled out a chair, and sat down.

He looked her in the eye and said, "You know what happened."

"How could I, Norm?"

"Stop, Kavitha. Just stop. You know we got hemmed up because of the murders. While D.C. Homicide dicks were investigating the double murder outside Congressional Cemetery they learned they had another body a couple of blocks away, a third victim shot in the head at point blank range. Afshar Ansary."

"What?" she gasped.

Norm slowly applauded her and then said, "You seem genuinely surprised. Excellent performance. Brava. 'All world's a stage and all the men and women merely players.'

"Now let's see if this surprises you: last night, you didn't replace the original Voynich with a fake, you replaced the fake with the real Voynich.

"There you go! *Now* you look genuinely surprised.

"When I worked Officer Thony's midnight shift, I locked the front door and had Luther come by and give me the same tools we used last night. He waited outside for me to return them.

"I compromised the cameras and case alarm and replaced the original Voynich with the fake one. I also went to Delta Deck and swiped the single most valuable book the Folger possesses, the last known copy of a quarto of *Titus Andronicus*, which I handed over to Von Essen along with his own copy of the Voynich. I got a writing table and handed it over to Rupert. Of course, they protested they didn't ask me to steal those treasures, but what I handed over to them was enough for the felony charges of Cultural Property Theft to stick, and the video I had of Rupert threatening the lives of my children was more than enough evidence for the felony charges of Conspiracy to Commit Murder. I'd already cut a deal with criminal justice personnel, like we discussed when we first went to Luther's office. I had Luther bring them to the Folger on January 20th and we discussed the case in the Shakespeare Gallery. At that meeting Daniel Marlowe, Deputy Director of the U.S. Marshals Service, swore me in as a special deputy, making me an officer of the court, and an integral component of this major criminal investigation.

"Still, I knew that even with all the felony charges facing them, the lives of you, my children, and me would still be in danger. That's why I set the meeting in Congressional Cemetery. If you hadn't mentioned the tall building in the distance, I would have brought up D.C. General Hospital. And then I would have mentioned Afshar Ansary in the same breath, just like I did after you asked about the tall building. I knew that you knew Ansary. I had Luther assign some of his operatives to tail the people who were tailing us so I could get the skinny on them.

"I counted on you telling Afshar Ansary to set up on the roof of the old D.C. General Hospital, so he could pick off Rupert and Richter when police took them into custody and walked them out of the cemetery past the Gatehouse. If I were a sniper, that's where I'd post.

"And I made sure that you were free to maneuver so you could get the job done by telling you to stay at the Folger until after midnight so you would be safe, rather than insisting that you come along, so you'd have elbow room to make your move."

She said, "You played me. You got me to do what you couldn't."

"I trusted you to be you."

"I figure you told Ansary that Rupert was working for Richter aka Von Essen, and that they had taken Johnson off the board, for whatever reason. Something like that. And then you killed Ansary after he took them off the board. No loose ends.

"First rule of assassination: kill the assassin."

"How did you know I wouldn't tell him to take you out, too?"

Norman shrugged and said, "I asked myself, what would killing me profit you? I couldn't come up with a reason why you should, so I took a chance."

"Is that the only reason for my not killing you that you could come up with?"

Kavitha pulled out another chair and sat down. She reached across the table for Norman's hand, but he slowly pulled it away.

"Did you have to sleep with Ansary? Like you had to with me?"

"No!" Kavitha snapped.

Norman conceded, "Okay, okay, that was below the belt." He sighed, reflected for a moment, and then said, "Don't get me wrong, Kavitha, I approve of what you did. It *had* to be done and I appreciate it..."

"But," she said.

Norman nodded and then said, "You and me just wouldn't work out, Kavitha. You know it and so do I. When you made your move with Ansary, to arrange for him to open fire on Whyte and Von Essen from a distance, you put a lot of people in harm's way, including me. Anyone of us near the targets could have been collateral damage. But that would have been an acceptable sacrifice for you to make in order to win.

"Sometimes the best moves require sacrifice, especially when it comes down to you or me. In the end, it will always be you."

Kavitha got up, walked around to his side of the table, leaned in, and kissed him passionately.

"I like you, Norm. Are you sure we can't *try* to work it out?"

"I like you, too," he said. "But you and me don't have a chance. Besides, my heart just isn't in it."

Kavitha nodded and then walked out of the kitchen and into the living room. He heard her favorite U2 song, *With or Without You*, coming from his stereo.

He heard the door of the coat closet in the foyer open and then close.

She was wearing her coat and her purse was hung from her left shoulder when she returned to the kitchen, suitcase in hand. She shrugged and said, "I packed last night." She smiled nervously and then continued, "I bought you this CD. Just a little something to remember me by. Happy Valentine's Day."

She walked over and put her copy of his house keys on the table, smiled and said, "You're, wrong, Norman. You *are* a teacher, and a good one. And your life has been well spent.

"Take care, Splenda Daddy."

Norm smiled and said, "Likewise, Junior. And thank you."

Kavitha sashayed out of the kitchen. He heard her say goodbye to Bruno and then he heard the front door open and close.

He walked into the living room and over to Bruno, who was standing at the picture window with his nose pressed to the glass, whining.

Norman Blalock and his dog looked out the window while Kavitha Netram's favorite U2 song played on.

[0000]

As Kavitha strolled down East Capitol Street, away from Norman's house, she listened to Donny Hathaway's *A Song For You* through the earbuds of her iPod.

She did not care if anyone saw her weeping.

The End

Luke 12:2

For there is nothing covered that shall not be revealed; neither hid, that shall not be known.

PRAISE FOR GUARDING SHAKESPEARE

"Peterson's novel is a lush tale of noir fiction in the spirit of the appealing thief utilizing all his wits against almost insurmountable odds."

– Literary Fiction Book Review

"Guarding Shakespeare hits all the right notes when it comes to keeping the reader guessing as to the final outcome, it's also very successful in mixing grittier moments with lighter elements, though not in a way that deflates intrigue or tension. Added to sharp, well nuanced dialogue and an eclectic mix of characters, Peterson has delivered a genuine page turner."

– Book Viral

"The most beautiful part of Guarding Shakespeare is the immense amount of detail and history pertaining to The Folger Shakespeare Library, and Shakespeare's own history, that Peterson weaves into this novella. When reading, you feel as though you're standing in the library yourself, looking around at each room. The novella is a thriller, yet it offers exquisite detail and information that you will carry with you forever.

"This thriller has the perfect combination of crime, mystery, and action, and you won't be able to turn the pages of this captivating novella fast enough."

– Red City Review

"Quintin Peterson's writing is one of those wonderful surprises: startlingly literary yet still gripping genre fiction."

– Austin S. Camacho, author of the bestselling Hannibal Jones Mystery Series

Norman Blalock will return in 𝕿𝖍𝖊 𝕾𝖍𝖆𝖐𝖊𝖘𝖕𝖊𝖆𝖗𝖊 𝕽𝖊𝖉𝖊𝖒𝖕𝖙𝖎𝖔𝖓

Ram Press

ABOUT THE AUTHOR

Quintin Peterson is the author of several plays and screenplays. He is a native Washingtonian.

As a junior high school student, he attended the Corcoran School of Art on a scholarship. While still in high school, he was honored with the University of Wisconsin's Science Fiction Writing Award, the National Council of Teachers of English Writing Award, and the Wisconsin Junior Academy's Writing Achievement Award.

As an undergraduate communications major at the University of Wisconsin, he wrote and performed in two plays for stage and videotape and received a Mary Roberts Rinehart Foundation grant for his play project, Change. A National Endowment for the Arts creative writing fellowship and a playwriting grant from the DC Commission on the Arts and Humanities followed. Subsequently, two of his radio plays were aired on WPFW-FM Pacifica Radio as productions of the Minority Arts Ensemble's Radio Drama Workshop '79.

Mr. Peterson was a police officer with the Metropolitan Police Department of Washington, D.C., for three decades, where he served for many years as media liaison officer and as the liaison between the department and members of the motion picture and television industries, acting as a script consultant and technical adviser. He also wrote and narrated training films for the police department. In December of 2010, he became an employee of the Folger Shakespeare Library's Department of Safety and Security.

An Active Member of Mystery Writers of America, Police Writers, and the Public Safety Writers Association (PSWA), he is the author of a book of poetry, **Nativity**; four crime novels, **SIN, The Wages of SIN**, **Guarding Shakespeare**, and its sequel, **The Voynich Gambit**; and is a contributor to six anthologies, *D.C. Noir*, edited by George Pelecanos, *Bad Cop, No Donut*, edited by John L. French; *From Shadows and Nightmares*, edited by Amber L. Campbell; *To Hell in a Fast Car*, edited by John L. French, *Explosions*, edited by Scott Bradley, and *Felons, Flames and Ambulance Rides*, edited by Marilyn Olsen. His short stories are also featured in the British horror magazine **SANITARIUM**, and *Heater* Magazine (formerly known as *eNoir*.) A short story version of *Guarding Shakespeare* is featured in *eNoir* Issue No. 2. Also, Folger Library Special Police Officer Quintin Peterson aka "the Bard Guard" is featured in the January 2017 Issue of American Theatre Magazine's *Role Call: 6 Theatre Workers You Should Know* column, in recognition of his security work at the Folger Theatre.

www.ingramcontent.com/pod-product-compliance
Lightning Source LLC
Chambersburg PA
CBHW032019170626
46807CB00006B/2878